I'M GLAD I DID

I'M GLAD I DID

Cynthia Weil

Published in the United States by Soho Teen an imprint of
Soho Press, Inc.
853 Broadway
New York, NY 10003

Library of Congress Cataloging-in-Publication Data

Weil, Cynthia.
I'm glad I did / Cynthia Weil.

HC ISBN 978-1-61695-356-0
PB ISBN 978-1-61695-574-8
eISBN 978-1-61695-357-7

1. Composers—Fiction. 2. Popular music—Fiction. 3. Internship
programs—Fiction. 4. Love—Fiction. 5. Secrets—Fiction.
6. Mystery and detective stories. I. Title.
PZ7.1.W43Im 2015
[Fic—dc23   2014025047

Interior design by Janine Agro, Soho Press, Inc.

Printed in the United States of America

10 9 8 7 6 5 4 3 2 1

This book is dedicated to my aunt, the late Toni Mendez. She was a dancer, a choreographer, a literary agent, and the family rebel. I idolized her. She was a woman ahead of her time who understood me before anyone else did, and who always said: "Cyn, dear, you have a book in you." Of course, she said that to everyone, including the doorman and the doctor about to perform surgery on her, but I know she always meant it, especially when she said it to me. So, Toni, here it is!

Prologue

Some people follow their destiny by accident. Take Dorothy in *The Wizard of Oz*. I was nine when I first saw the movie, and as soon as Dorothy sang "Somewhere Over the Rainbow," I knew she'd find a way to get there. True, she didn't do anything to make it happen; a tornado just happened to take her exactly where she needed to go. But somehow that song still made me believe she had something to do with it.

Knowing my life was not a movie, that there wasn't much chance of a tornado in New York City, and that the place I needed to go was only across town, I knew I'd have to get there by myself. So way back then, before I even hit a double-digit birthday, I made a decision. One day I would fly over my own rainbow and write a song like that one. A song that could make people believe in possibilities and dreams. One day I'd walk through those big brass doors of the Brill Building at 1619 Broadway, the place where my Uncle Bernie told me songs were "born," and I'd make it to Oz, too.

It wasn't until seven years later, the summer of 1963, that I was able to figure out how to get there. And even though I may have done it on my own and faced my fear by choice, looking back now, it seems that most of what followed—the joy and the love, the tragedy and the loss, the craziness of it all—was meant to be. It was my destiny that summer to find out who my family was, who my friends were, and eventually, who I was.

The only part that didn't feel like destiny and never will was the cost.

CHapTer ONe

There are three unbreakable rules in my family.
1. The Greens always have breakfast together.
2. The Greens always negotiate instead of arguing.
3. The Greens always become lawyers.

I'm hardly ever hungry at breakfast, and while I really love a good screaming argument (I believe it clears the air), I've managed to live with rules one and two. It's rule number three that scares me, crushes my dreams and destroys my soul. The truth, the whole truth, and nothing but the truth, is that I do not now, nor have I ever wanted to be an attorney.

Unlike my big brother Jeffrey, I have not inherited the legal gene. Jeff—who at the age of seven suggested a contractual relationship between us regarding use of the bathroom we shared—is clearly a Green. I was four at the time, so I accepted, proof only that I seem to have been born into the wrong family. If I didn't look so much like my mother, I'd suspect I'd been adopted, but we have the same face (heart shaped), same hair (ridiculously straight, medium brown with red highlights) and the same big feet (don't even ask what size).

That morning in June, I had a bigger secret than my shoe size.

What I was keeping under wraps was a plan to break sacred rule number three by getting a summer job in the music business. A job that would no doubt lead to a total family flip-out. I had no intention of telling them anything about it unless I got it. Today was just an interview. I was painfully aware, though, that if anyone in my family of legal eagles thought I was hiding something, I was going to be cross-examined, so I tried to look relaxed and extremely normal as I ambled into the dining room and slid into my chair.

"Good morning, Irving," Jeff greeted me, munching on cornflakes. "You look a little more uptight than usual. What's up?"

So much for my acting ability. My brother has called me Irving, as in Irving Berlin, ever since I was idiot enough to tell him that I wanted to write songs.

"Stop calling your sister Irving," my mother instructed. She was cutting off the top of her egg with my grandmother's silver egg cutter, reading the *Herald Tribune* and monitoring our conversation at the same time. She was one of the few people in the world who could do three things at once and do all of them perfectly.

My mother, Janice Green—Janny—is a criminal attorney. My dad, Julius Green—Jules—is a judge. Jeff, the bathroom negotiator, is pre-law at Columbia. He's also working at

Janny's office for the summer. Could he be more perfect? J is the family letter, given the happy coincidence of my parents' first names. But J can also stand for lots of other things like "judgmental." Or "joyless." Or "just not understood."

Janny and Jules named me Justice, and if that's not making a point and giving a kid vocational guidance, I don't know what is. My middle name is Jeanette after Jeanette Rankin, who was the first woman to serve in the United States Congress. Try living up to that. The only saving grace is that everyone calls me JJ. I hardly ever tell anyone my real name or why I got it. Nobody knows at Dalton where I graduated from high school last week, class of 1963. I'm sixteen, two years younger than most of my friends because I skipped a grade in elementary school and made one up in middle school rapid advance.

I mention this as proof that I am not too dumb to be a lawyer. I simply don't want to be one. I've known what I wanted to be ever since I was three years old and crawled up on the piano bench in my family's living room. Ever since I touched the keys and realized I could make my own sound. Ever since I heard the Latin music that Juana (another cruel letter J coincidence), our housekeeper, played on her radio. I've wanted to be a music maker, a spinner of dreams, the creator of some kind of new and beautiful noise, a poetic voice saying what others feel but can't express.

The problem is that in the Green family, saying you want to be a songwriter is the equivalent of saying you want to be an axe murderer—or even worse, a music business lowlife who rips people off, like my Uncle Bernie.

Juana whispered, "*Buenos días, cariña,*" and placed my usual toasted bran muffin in front of me.

"Justice, I think you're going a little heavy on the mascara," Janny observed. "It makes you look unhappy."

"It's not mascara, Mom, they're false eyelashes. Everyone's wearing them."

"You are not everyone," Jules reminded me from behind *The New York Times.* He peered over the headline JFK SIGNS EQUAL PAY ACT. "Your mother's right. You look unhappy."

"It's her guilty look," Jeff chimed in. "I remember it from when we shared a bathroom and she used it during my time."

"Why are you talking about me as if I'm not here, Jeffrey?" I asked calmly. Whenever he did that, I wanted to rip out his vocal chords, but letting him know would mean he'd won. So I smoothed the skirt of my seersucker shirtwaist dress and smiled. "Don't you think that type of behavior is rude, Mom?"

"JJ has a point, Jeffrey. You two could debate it, but it's getting late, and I have to get to the office."

Janny stood and slipped into her raspberry linen suit jacket. It matched her pillbox hat perfectly. My mom looked like Jackie Kennedy before Jackie did. Impossibly chic. So chic that people often took her for a model. She was also brilliant, charming, well read, successful—and one of only two women in her class at Columbia law. You might say she was a tough act to follow, or you might say it was better not to try. You might also say that trying to slip into the music business on her watch had to be a death wish.

Jules shrugged into his jacket, folded *The New York Times,* which he always finished before breakfast, and handed it to Janny. "Check Earl Wilson's column," he told her. "It appears Bernie is being called to testify in some payola scheme again."

"What else is new?" Janny asked, biting her lip. "I say a prayer every night—"

"That no one will figure out that 'the godfather of the music business' is your no-goodnik brother," Jules finished. "We know, Janny, we know."

"I know you know. I don't know why I'm compelled to repeat myself." She dropped her keys into her handbag and the newspaper into her attaché. Then she turned her attention to something she actually could control: us. "Justice, as discussed, you have this week to find a summer job doing something useful, or I'll expect you to begin filing down at my office next Monday. Being around a law office might awaken your legal instincts. Jeff, there's a package you need to pick up at Malken, Malken and Strobe. Please get it to me before ten thirty, and then Susan will tell you what to do today. Jules, I'd like to share a cab with you if you're ready to leave."

And with that everyone jumped to do Janny's bidding, as everyone usually did. I hightailed it out of her sight before she could figure out that Jeff was right on the money, that I was guilty as charged. Today I was taking a giant step toward my not-so-secret dream and my parents' worst nightmare. Today I was sticking my toe into what Janny called "that cesspool, the music business." Defying her was scary enough. But even more terrifying would be learning if I had any right to my dream. Today I'd be finding out if I had any songwriting talent.

CHAPTER TWO

I stood at the corner of West Forty-Ninth and Broadway, clutching my purse and staring up at Oz itself, the Brill Building. I silently offered up my own Janny-like prayer that I wouldn't run into "no-goodnik" Uncle Bernie, even though I wasn't sure we'd even recognize each other. I hadn't seen him since I was a kid.

This was it, the Mecca of songwriting. The brass doors were flanked by black marble pillars. Above them, set into a brass niche, was the bust of a young guy. I always thought it was George Gershwin or some other famous songwriter, but I found out it was the developer's son. The poor guy died at seventeen. His name wasn't even Brill. The Brill brothers owned the land, and they leased it to a developer. The Brills actually had a clothing store on the main floor.

How do I know all this? I know it because I did a report on New York architecture for my art class just so I could research this location. I can also tell you more than you want to know about the New York Public Library. Like the lions out front were named Patience and Fortitude by Mayor LaGuardia in the 1930s.

A steady stream of people poured in and out of those amazing doors, and all I'd ever wanted was to have a legitimate reason to be one of them. Fumbling in my purse, I pulled out the scrap I'd torn from last week's *Cashbox*:

WANTED: Good Music Publishing seeks smart assistant/talented aspiring songwriter. Exchange office work for feedback on songs from hot publisher. Call Rona at Ju5-5253 for audition appointment.

I took a deep breath.

I belong here, I told myself for the thousandth time. *This job fits me like a glove.*

And I was already planning to emphasize the office experience to Janny and Jules.

Shoving the scrap back in my bag, I checked my watch, then strode through the entrance. I wanted to be early, but not so early that I looked desperate.

Inside, everything was gleaming brass and mirrors. I double-checked the Good Music suite number and strolled as casually as I could to the elevator at the end of the lobby.

A whole bunch of people, mostly men in suits, stood waiting. The only person close to my age was a really cute guy. He looked like he might be Italian, with olive skin and black hair. He was studying papers in a manila folder, and when he looked up at the elevator dial, I saw that his eyes were green. Not blue-green or gray-green but almost emerald green. I'd never seen anything like them before. I had to look away to get my mind back on my own business, reviewing my song in my head, the one I was going to play for my audition.

When the doors opened the waiting crowd, including Green Eyes, swarmed into the elevator. Everyone yelled out their floors to the elevator operator, a short cheery guy in a uniform, and I chirped out, "Eight," hoping I'd been heard.

Conversations swirled around me as the doors opened and closed.

"Hey, Nick, when you take a break, bring me up the trades."

"Sure thing, Mr. Bienstock," the elevator guy answered.

"Where are you this week, Aaron?"

"Five with a bullet, *Cashbox*. Seven with a bullet, *Billboard*."

"Enjoy it now, my friend. Goodman's got the follow-up."

"Is there anything he doesn't have the follow-up to?"

"I've heard he's asking for a guarantee of the B side these days, and he's getting it."

"Yeah, it's that and your firstborn child."

There were some chuckles. I wondered what was so funny. They were speaking in Music-Biz, and the only person I knew who could translate was Uncle Bernie. But soon I wouldn't need an interpreter. I'd learn how to speak fluent Music-Biz on my own.

When we hit eight, I elbowed my way out of the elevator.

Good Music was way down at the end of the hall, and as I made my way there, I could hear muffled music coming from behind closed doors: pianos pounding out riffs, voices struggling to find melodies and records being played—no, not played, blasted. All of it was punctuated by some very bad language. I quickened my pace with a secret smile. It was exactly how I imagined it, raw and real, and a million light-years away from the world of the Green family.

At Good Music I entered a small waiting room with built-in seating. Two guys a little older than me had settled in, probably to wait for *their* auditions. One was tall and skinny, all elbows, knees, and acne. The other was a chubby little guy with an already receding hairline, wearing a suit and a tie with musical notes on it. At the far end, a switchboard operator was busy chewing gum and frantically answering continuous incoming calls.

"Good Music. Hi, Nancy, Bobby said to tell Mr. Wexler he'll call him back after lunch. Good Music. Sorry, Mr. Goodman is booked all week. Just drop off the demo, and I'll get it to his secretary. Good Music. Please hold. Good Music. We're not seeing any more applicants until Friday, so call back on Thursday to see if the job's still open. Good Music. Sorry . . ." She looked up at me. "Lost the hold. So what can I do for ya?"

"I'm JJ Green. I have an eleven o'clock appointment to see Mr. Goodman about the assistant job."

She nodded. "Take a load off. You're after these guys."

As I sat down, she called out, "Paul Keller, go on in."

The suit with the musical tie got up and gulped audibly. All the color drained out of his face. He looked so terrified that my heart went out to him, even though we were competing for the same job.

"Good luck," I whispered.

He looked at me, eyes glazed with fear, wiped his hands on his pants and entered the inner office. He looked as if he was going to his execution.

"You're not here for the assistant job, are you?" the skinny one asked.

"Yeah, I am."

"I didn't know girls wrote songs," he announced, as if his ignorance was something to be proud of.

"We learn something every day, don't we?" I responded politely. "Did you ever hear of Alberta Hunter?"

His face was blank.

"Great blues songwriter, female. Wrote a song called 'Downhearted Blues' that sold two million in 1923. How about Kay Swift?"

He smirked. "I know about Bob Swift. He was a catcher for the Detroit Tigers way back."

"Kay Swift was the first woman to write the whole score to a Broadway musical called *Fine and Dandy* in 1930. Did you ever—"

"Hey, you a music teacher's apprentice or something?"

Before I could answer, Paul Keller of the musical tie emerged from the inner office. He stood facing us in a daze.

"He hated my song," he announced in a bewildered voice. "Bobby hated the best song I ever wrote. It made my mother cry." He stared at us. "He's mean—really, really mean." Before we could respond, he blew his nose loudly into a crumpled Kleenex and exited.

The receptionist nodded our way. "Artie Lorber."

Tall-and-Skinny got up and stood there for a moment, his eyes wide with the same panic. You could almost hear the wheels in his brain turning. He hesitated for what seemed like an eternity, then turned and followed Paul Keller's route out of the office.

"Wrong door," the receptionist called out.

But Artie Lorber paid no attention. He didn't even look back.

"We lose a few of the thin-skinned ones," she muttered. "Go on in . . ." She checked her list. "JJ Green."

I stood up, took a deep breath and moved toward the door that Artie couldn't open. *Here goes,* I thought. *Be brave, be strong, and be ready to hear the truth.*

CHAPTER THREE

The room I walked into was five times larger than the room I came from. At the far end, guarding a red lacquered door emblazoned with BOBBY GOODMAN in gold letters, was a cute girl. She wasn't much older than me, and she was wearing a beige polka-dot Anne Fogarty dress that I'd been saving my birthday money to buy. On her desk was a brass nameplate: RONA CALUCCI: DON'T TRY TO GET PAST ME. She was talking on the phone, rummaging through a huge stack of music paper and trying to wipe up spilled coffee all at the same time. There were more doors leading off this main room, and from behind them I could hear more pianos in different keys, hammering out clashing melodies.

I took out my handkerchief—Janny always insisted I carry a real handkerchief and not a Kleenex—and tried to help with the mopping-up operation.

Rona looked up at me. "Thanks," she said. "You JJ?"

"That's me," I answered.

"First female applicant." She took my soggy handkerchief, squeezed it into the wastepaper basket and handed
it back to me. "Go on in."

I walked into the vast office. There was a baby grand
piano and a huge desk with records and tapes scattered
all over. Behind it sat the man himself, Bobby Goodman.

He was a big guy. Not fat, just big. I would have guessed
him to be early thirties, but I had read in *Cashbox* he was
only twenty-four. His face was wide and open, with a high
forehead and thinning hair. He was wearing a short-sleeved
shirt. You never would have guessed by looking at him that
he was a big deal music publisher. He looked more like a
coach for a suburban Little League baseball team.

Taking my application from a stack on his desk, he
leaned back in his chair. "So, JJ, what makes you want to
learn about the music business?"

I sat down in the chair facing him and tried not to sound
as nervous as I was. "Well, I want to be a songwriter. I'm
sixteen, and I've been playing the piano since I was about
four. I took a semester of lessons in school, but I'm mostly
self-taught. I started writing songs when I was ten, but you
definitely don't want to hear any of those." I chuckled self-
consciously.

Bobby didn't even pretend to smile. A sense of humor
was obviously not one of his character traits. "What made
you start writing? Anyone in your family musical?"

"Oh, no, nobody, not a soul. Everyone's a lawyer."

An image of Uncle Bernie popped up in my mind, but I
ignored it. I was determined to get this job on my own. No
Bernie bias would influence anyone's decision.

"So are you the black sheep or the shining star?"

I almost smiled. "Definitely the black sheep."

"You're in high school, right?"

"I graduated last week."

"You must be smart," Bobby observed. "You going to college?"

"Yeah, I got into Barnard, but I could work part-time after school in the fall if you wanted me to."

"I got it." He leaned back and closed his eyes. "Now play me something you wrote. Play me a song you've written that should be recorded."

The last bit caught me off guard. I had never thought about getting my songs recorded. I just wrote what I liked. But wasn't that what I was here for? My heart was pounding like a bass drum as I sat down, but once my fingers touched the keys, I was home.

The song was called "We Will Rise." I had written it only last week, so it was fresh in my mind and my fingers. I wanted to write something idealistic. The feel came from a folk song I loved that Pete Seger sang called "We Shall Overcome." My song was proud with similar gospel chord changes and lots of passing tones. The words of my first verse went:

> We will rise like the morning sun.
> We will rise when we stand as one,
> For the wounded and the weak,
> For the ones who cannot speak,
> For the old with no choices,
> Children whose voices cry in the bitter night.

For those chained by the heartless,
Souls in the darkness longing to see the light
We will rise.

I tried not to let my nerves make me speed up. I made believe I was playing just for me, and when I did that, I actually thought it sounded pretty good.

When I finished, there was dead silence.

I looked at Bobby. His eyes were still closed. "What else do you have that you think I could pitch?" he asked without opening them.

That shook me up. I'd only rehearsed one song. My mind went blank. I had never heard the word *pitch* before used in this way, but I could guess what he meant. He wasn't talking baseball. He wanted a song he could play for a record company. A song to show him I was worth hiring.

Then I remembered one I'd written a year ago called "Where Would I Be." I had fallen in love with the score *How to Succeed in Business Without Really Trying,* and my favorite song was "I Believe in You." It was a love song, but the character, J. Pierrepont Finch, sang it to himself in the mirror. I tried to write a pop song that did the same thing, that made sense as a song you could sing to yourself or someone else. I wanted it to have the same kind of lilt and drive and humor as "I Believe in You." I wasn't sure many pop songs had any humor, but why not try to write one?

It started with the chorus, but I played it out of tempo so it almost sounded like an intro until the tempo picked up. I had to concentrate hard to remember the words.

Once I began, though, they came rolling off my tongue. I made believe I was looking at myself in the mirror like J. Pierrepont Finch.

Where would I be if I didn't have you?
I hope I never find out,
As you can guess, I'd be a mess
I'm positive without a doubt.
I'd be behind the eight ball in fetal position,
Out of my mind and out of commission,
I'd be without hope, at the end of my rope.
You might say I'd be up a tree
'Cause if I didn't have you, nowhere is where I would be.

It was hard not to speed up, and my hands got kind of clammy, but I made it through without a major screw-up. Then I sat there, heart still pounding, listening to the loudest silence of all time.

Finally Bobby sighed. He opened his eyes and looked straight at me. "You don't listen to the radio, do you?" It was a statement in the form of a question. He didn't wait for an answer. "You listen to folk music and go to Broadway musicals, right? You need direction lyrically. If you want to write pop songs, forget complicated ideas. Don't try to be funny. I can't get records on inspirational songs with inner rhymes or lyrics that sound like something out of a musical comedy. You need to write words that come from your heart and can touch the hearts of other girls your age. Write about how you feel. Write about love."

I opened my mouth and then closed it. Love? What did I know about love?

"Do your homework," Bobby continued. "Listen to the radio. Listen to Cousin Brucie and Murray the K. Learn the Top Ten songs well enough to play them backward and forward. Study grooves, chord progressions, and ideas. You need to remember three things: Simple, simple, simple. Thanks for coming in." He stood up and held out his hand.

I took it, fighting back tears. "Thanks for your time," I mumbled and sprinted for the door.

"How'd it go?" asked Rona as I raced past her.

I shook my head and bolted through the inner sanctum and reception area. Out in the hall, I allowed myself to cry as I leaned on the elevator button. Fortunately, when the doors opened, the elevator was empty except for Nick, the operator. My nose was leaking along with my eyes. My handkerchief was a soggy, coffee-stained mess, so when Nick handed me a Kleenex, I took it gratefully.

"Hey, who did what to make a cute kid like you cry those big tears?" he asked sympathetically.

"Bobby Goodman," I told him between sobs. "He basically told me I'm an untalented idiot."

"Not a good feeling."

"No, my mother'll be happy, though. She doesn't want me to be a songwriter. She hates the music business."

"Most mothers do. What does she know?"

"A lot." I sniffed, then shoved the Kleenex in my pocket, trying to regain some composure as the elevator descended. "Her brother is the godfather of the music business."

"Bernie Rubin?"

"That's him."

We reached the lobby. Nick hesitated before he opened the door. "I don't want to open up until you're okay," he said.

"I'm as okay as I'm gonna be. I won't have to tell my family anything now. Nobody knew I was applying for this job. I'll just have to go to work for my mother this summer. Good for me." The thought sent more tears rolling down my cheeks.

Nick sighed. "Listen, kid, there's one thing I know for sure: ya never know what's gonna happen, so save the tears for when you really need 'em. You may be wasting them today."

It was such a sweet thing to say—and he was such an unlikely guy to say it—that I dried my eyes and almost smiled.

"Good for you, kiddo," Nick said, smiling back. He pulled the door open with a flourish.

aFTer wanDerInG THe STreeTS for a few hours in a fog of self-pity, I finally shambled home at two o'clock. Juana was the only person in the apartment, of course. I strolled past her nonchalantly and headed for my bedroom. But she'd caught a glimpse of my face, and in less than a minute she was knocking on my door.

"Go away, please," I pleaded.

Today she chose not to listen. She opened the door and sat down beside me on the bed, which for some reason opened the floodgates again. She didn't even ask what was wrong, just patted my back, and when I sat up, she pulled me close. Now I realized what she'd known all along: I needed unconditional comfort. The smell of her cologne and the softness of her pale coffee skin had consoled me for as long as I could remember—and it still did. Whenever I was upset, she always spoke to me in English, even though I spoke Spanish fluently. It was her way of reaching out.

"Tell me, *cariña*," she whispered.

"I thought I had talent, but I don't." My voice was hoarse. Saying the words out loud didn't help either. "Someone who really knows told me my songs aren't simple enough, and my words aren't any good."

"I don't know anything about talent, *mi niña*," she said softly, "but I know this is not the only time you will be disappointed. It hurts not to get what you want, but sometimes you learn from it."

"You don't understand," I told her. "I write too complicated. I don't know a hit, and my lyrics aren't—"

The phone rang. I pulled away and hurried to the living room, grateful for the interruption.

"Hello." I sniffled.

"May I speak to JJ, please?"

"This is JJ."

"Hi, this is Rona at Good Music." She paused. "Are you okay?"

This was such a loaded question that when I tried to answer, nothing came out.

"Congratulations, JJ," Rona continued in the silence. "You got the job."

"I got the what?" The room seemed to swirl around me. I wasn't sure what I felt, other than disbelief. This had to be a mistake.

"You got the assistant gig. We're sending over a three-month contract for the songwriting part. The messenger will be there within the hour. Your parents have to sign since you're under twenty-one. Bobby wants you to start Monday at ten, so bring the signed contract with you when you come in."

"I really got the job?"

"Abso-elvis-lutely."

"But . . . but . . . I don't understand . . ."

"It's what we say around here when someone asks an obvious question. Just be here Monday," Rona cut in. "Ten o'clock. See ya." Before she slammed the phone down, I heard her yelling, "Bobby's in a meeting. Don't touch that door, Steve."

Grinning through my tears, I dropped the phone back on the hook.

Juana rushed up to me. "¿Qué pasó?"

"This is really, really crazy, but I got the job."

The worried look disappeared from her face. "Mira, you learned something from this," she whispered as she hugged me. "You learned not to cry too soon."

Laughing, I hugged her back. "You're the second person who told me that today," I confessed. I was happier than I thought possible, but I couldn't help wondering what could have made Bobby change his mind. Were the ones after me so bad that my songs began to sound good? Was it worth trying to figure out?

Couldn't I just accept it and be happy?

Of course not. I would never take a "yes" for an answer without knowing why it had changed from a "no." I was, after all, a Green.

CHapTer Four

I waited as long as I possibly could before spilling the beans. After dinner when Janny and Jules were relaxing in the living room, I retrieved my contract from my bedroom. Jeff, of course, chose this night to stick around. He knew something was up long before our parents had finished their coffee and were sloshing brandy around in snifters. I'd changed for dinner into an elegant red Anne Klein sheath that Janny had loved and bought for me and reapplied lipstick to match. No fake lashes either.

Once I was sure the liquor had taken effect, and Jules was smoking his after-dinner Marlboro, I sat down, papers in hand.

"I have a summer job," I announced. Best to start with the good news.

"JJ, dear, that's wonderful," Janny enthused. "Truthfully, I was hoping you'd end up working for me, but congratulations. Isn't that wonderful, Jules?"

"Wonderful," echoed my dad, exhaling a cloud of smoke. "Tell us all about it."

I took a deep breath. I was sitting so close to the edge of my seat, I thought I'd fall off. "Before I do, I want to ask you something. Mom, did you have any idea where I was going today?"

She laughed. "I'm an attorney, Justice, not a detective. You never told me where you were going, so obviously I didn't know."

"So you never said anything to Bernie?"

"Bernie?" Her tone changed. The glaze over her eyes evaporated, replaced by a focused stare. She sat up straight and placed her brandy on its coaster. "This is not headed in a good direction." She shot Jules a *pay attention* glance, then zeroed in on me. "You know I haven't spoken to him in six years, not since—"

"Not since he showed up uninvited to Jeff's bar mitzvah," I finished.

"Exactly." Janny's voice became tense. "Your uncle is a gambler, a thief, and a music business lowlife. Why would I want to speak to him about anything?"

"Now don't get worked up," Jules cautioned. "You're not telling us you got a job in the music business, are you, Justice?"

"That's exactly what I'm telling you," I said, trying not to get defensive. "And I wanted to be sure that Uncle Bernie wasn't involved because I want to make my own way on my own talent. At first it seemed like I didn't get the job. But then I got it, and I can't figure out why, and I just thought maybe . . ." I ran out of breath and stopped.

"There is no way Bernie heard about it from us," Janny snapped. "Since this is the first *we've* heard of it. And now I want to know where you were, who you saw, and everything about them."

"Uh-oh," Jeff commented, choosing this moment to make his presence felt. He'd made sure he sat down out of the range of fire, but close enough so he could observe my agony.

"The company is called Good Music," I told them. "And they publish songs and produce records."

"There was an article about them in last week's *Wall Street Journal*," Jules remarked. "They've only been in business three years, but they're doing very well."

I nodded, hoping this was a sign of encouragement. "They're really hot—I mean successful—and I'll be doing office work, but I'll also have the chance to listen to the writers who are getting songs recorded. I'll be playing my own songs for Bobby Goodman, the head of the company. There's a chance I could even get a song recorded."

"So, JJ," Janny cut in sharply, "knowing how I feel about the music business, you went behind my back and applied for a job at a music publisher."

"Not exactly," I protested weakly. "If you had asked, I would have told you, but you didn't ask."

"What's done is done," Jules declared. He stubbed out his cigarette, looked at my mother and then back at me. "Justice, your obsession with songwriting has always bewildered us. If it's a hobby, that's one thing . . . but you know it's not any serious kind of occupation. Frankly, I don't condone what you did and how you did it, but I for one would like to see you get it out of your system. This job may be just the way to do that."

Janny was already shaking her head. "I don't agree, Jules," she said. "I'm inclined to say no to the whole thing. It's not just the job. It's the deception on JJ's part."

My heart stopped. I felt completely out of control, which I was. After all, they were already talking about me in the third person, which they knew I hated, as if I were a criminal waiting to be sentenced.

"And what is that in your hand, JJ?" Janny demanded.

I took another deep breath, knowing the worst was yet to come. "It's a contract for three months. It says Good Music owns the publishing rights to any songs that I write during that time, whether they get recorded or not."

"Think you'll get a record, Irving?" Jeff asked.

I turned to him, my gaze steely. "I don't know," I told him, annoyed that he was sticking his nose into this at all.

"Let me take a look," Janny ordered.

I handed her the contract. As she flipped through it, nobody dared to breathe audibly. The clock on the wall boomed in synch with my heart. When my mother looked up, she shook her head.

"This is a terrible contract. It's very one-sided in the publisher's favor. I would advise against this deal, Justice, for anyone, let alone my own daughter."

"Mom," I said, trying to keep my voice from shaking, "I'm going to be honest with you. I don't really care if the contract's good or bad. I can learn so much there. It's where I want to be this summer. Please just sign it. Please. It's like Dad said—this way I can get it out of my system."

My mother didn't answer. I could see the cogs turning in her brain. She was mentally reviewing arguments for and against. Then she and Jules turned to each other once more in silent consultation. My future hung in the air like the last cloud of Jules's cigarette smoke.

Suddenly Jeff stood up. "I have a solution," he offered. "It's only for three months, right? So let Irving do it. But if she doesn't get one of her songs recorded by the time it's over, she has to give up this crazy songwriting thing and never mention it again."

My eyes narrowed. I couldn't figure out if he was trying to help me or hurt me. My brother has always had a weird instinctive ability to understand our parents in a way I never have. When he and I fought as kids—as in actual kicking and punching—he somehow knew they would never intervene. Even when he pinned me to the floor, and it was clear I couldn't win, they insisted we work out our disagreements ourselves. Finally, when I was ten, I begged Janny to sign me up for Brazilian jujitsu classes (Juana actually told me about it) because it was all about ground fighting. She was happy to do it, even though I was the only girl in the class. But I was such a klutz that after all my classes I only mastered one move, the upward lift escape. By then Jeff had stopped attacking me physically and had moved on to verbal assault. And that, of course, made his suggestion right now scarier.

"Hmm," Janny mused, rolling Jeff's proposition around in her meticulous mind.

I had to hand it to Jeff: I could tell the thought of never having to hear me talk about songwriting again had made an impact on Janny. Her lips curved up in a little smile. "Would you agree to that, JJ?" she asked. "I might actually let you do this if you promised that it could be a way to put an end to your songwriting fixation."

I shot Jeff a dirty look and turned back to my mother. "Why are you all so sure I won't get a record?"

"Because you're a Green," Jules proclaimed in his court-room voice. "You were born for the law."

That's how simple it was for them. They honestly believed that music was a decision I had made, like wanting to learn Brazilian jujitsu. But it wasn't. It was a part of me—like my laugh and big feet—like arguing was for them. I didn't know if I had talent. I didn't know if I would ever write a song worthy of being recorded. But I knew I had to have the chance to try.

Bobby himself had told me I didn't know what I was doing. A door had opened, and I had to walk through it. Maybe Jeff's deal was fair. If I couldn't get a song recorded this summer, maybe it would be a sign that I was on the wrong track. I didn't know how I'd go on living after that, but I'd worry about the future when it became the present.

"I'll do it," I said. "If a song of mine isn't recorded by the time I start school, I'll give up songwriting."

"Agreed," Janny and Jules announced, almost in unison.

Court adjourned, I thought with a mixture of terror and relief.

"Good luck, Irving," said Jeff with a wicked grin. "I'll be rooting for you."

CHAPTER FIVE

Two mornings later, at 9:50, I joined the crowd surging into the Brill Building. At this hour there was a more even mix of men and women; the secretaries were reporting for work. But there was another crucial difference. Today I really belonged. My dress, an olive-green linen Jonathan Logan shift with buttons on the shoulder, had been approved by Janny. Even if I was going to hell, my mother insisted that I go in style.

I was waiting for the elevator when I spotted him: Mr. Green Eyes. Once again he was engrossed in a sheaf of papers, waiting for the elevator. I snaked forward so that we pushed our way through the door together, shoulder to shoulder.

"Writer or publisher?" I asked, smiling my warmest smile.

He looked up for an instant with total disinterest. "Both," he answered, and dropped his eyes back to his paperwork.

I wanted to disappear into the background, but I'd wedged myself next to him, so I had to put up with being ignored until he got off at seven.

As it turned out, this little fiasco was pretty much an omen of things to come.

WHEN I WALKED IN to Good Music, the girl at the switchboard motioned me through the door into the big room. Rona was on the phone at her desk, but the second she saw me, she waved me over.

"I'll be sure to have Bobby get back to you," she purred sweetly into the mouthpiece. Then she slammed it down on the hook and snapped, "Sure I will, after I put my eyes out. What makes a writer think I'll get him in to see Bobby if he comes on to me? Ugh! I need a shower."

"It must be awful," I sympathized.

Rona sighed. "Yeah, but I get it in a crazy way. I'm Bobby's guard dog, and everyone wants to pet me. Writers will sell out their grandmothers to have their songs listened to by someone like Bobby, so why wouldn't they pretend to like his secretary?" She laughed at herself. "But enough about me. Let me show you the filing system. Pick up those lead sheets and follow me."

There were stacks of paper all over her desk. I stood still, bewildered.

"You don't know what a lead sheet is, do you?"

I shook my head.

She picked up a pile of music paper and stuck it in my arms. "Come with me, listen and learn. A lead sheet is a piece of music paper with the basic melody, chords and lyrics to a song written on it. The writers make out one for every song they write, and we make two copies and file one with the original. Then we send one to the copyright office in Washington. When I say 'we,' I mean 'you,' JJ. This is going to be your first responsibility, copying and filing lead sheets. Got it?"

"Got it," I answered, juggling the papers in one arm and saluting with the other with a smile.

"Very cute," Rona responded, but she smiled back.

She led me into a small room with a big copying machine and a load of file cabinets. After a few demonstrations, I was able to make a copy by myself.

Rona watched and nodded like a proud mama. "You *are* smart," she said, finally relaxing. "I knew it the minute I saw you. I really wanted another girl in the office. We are so outnumbered. There's Marilyn at the switchboard and me and two female writers, but there are at least a dozen guys, not even counting Bobby. It's such a pain when you get your period unexpectedly, and there are so few people to hit up for a tampon."

"I always have one on me," I volunteered.

She laughed. "I knew you would. You carry a handkerchief, for God's sake. You're the type who is prepared for everything in the classiest way possible. I had my fingers crossed that something would happen to change Bobby's mind about you. And then when Bernie called, my prayers were answered—"

"What?" I interrupted. I paused in mid-copy, nearly dropping the lead sheets in my hands. "Did Bernie Rubin speak to Bobby about me?"

Rona shot me a puzzled glance and hit the copy button for me. "Of course. Didn't you tell him to?"

"No, I absolutely did not." I answered, trying not to explode or cry even though I wanted to do both. "I never even told him I was coming up here to apply for this job. I haven't spoken to my uncle in years."

Rona shrugged. "Well, who did you tell? 'Cause Bernie knew everything. He told Bobby that he made you feel like an untalented idiot and he personally knew you were neither."

I blinked a few times. "How do you know he said that?"

"It just so happened that I didn't completely disconnect when he was talking to Bobby." She flashed a sly grin. "There's something wrong with my disconnect button sometimes."

I was hardly listening. "I don't know how he could have known," I said out loud. "I didn't tell anyone but my . . . oh, wait a minute. I did." It was all coming back to me. Especially the words *untalented idiot.* "The elevator guy, Nick. I told him."

"Well, mystery solved," Rona said, turning toward the filing cabinets. She sounded like she couldn't have cared less, not that I blamed her. "Bernie Rubin wants to know everything that's happening in the biz. He even pays the elevator operators when they give him valuable info. I bet Nick made twenty bucks for spilling the beans."

I swallowed hard. "Rona," I said, hoarsely, "you don't understand. I really wanted to get this on my own."

She glanced over her shoulder and arched an eyebrow. "And I really wanted to go to college. But I have to work here until I save enough money. You can't always get what you want."

"That sounds like a song title," I grumbled.

She laughed again. "Nah, too negative. Bobby likes positive songs. He told me he wants you listening to Top Forty radio all the time. It's okay to bring in a transistor radio if you don't play it too loud. Now," she announced, her voice all business again, "it's time to learn the filing system."

CHaPTer SIX

I was starving by my lunch break at one, but I had more important things to attend to.

I leaned on the elevator button, pretending it was Nick's throat, and prayed I'd get his car. There were only two elevators, so the odds were fifty-fifty. But sure enough, like everything else that day, it didn't work out for me. The other operator was a dapper Puerto Rican guy named Antonio, who I later found out was a ridiculously successful bookie. I pretended I'd forgotten something, waved it closed and pressed the button again.

Half a minute later, Nick opened the door. The elevator was jammed with people headed out for lunch, but I slid in anyway. Nick flashed a friendly smile at me and I nodded back, my lips tight. When everyone poured out into the lobby, I stayed put.

"I'm going back up," I told him, shooting daggers at him with my eyes. "And I'm in a hurry."

He didn't seem to notice. "Your private express," he said cheerily, closing the door and waiting for a floor number. "Where to, kiddo?"

"Tell me something," I demanded. "What made you think it was okay to tell Bernie Rubin all the private, confidential, secret, personal stuff I told you yesterday after my meeting with Bobby?"

His smile remained intact. He didn't even blink. "Well, first of all, you didn't tell me *not* to tell him," he responded smoothly. "Number two, I knew he could help you. And number three, I felt bad for you." He lowered his voice and placed a gloved hand on the elevator crank. "Was I wrong about any of those things?"

This was not going exactly as I had planned. I thought he'd be apologizing all over the place for betraying a confidence. "No, but I wanted to get the job without any help," I countered. I was starting to feel like a broken record, appropriate considering my location.

"Trust me, kiddo, that wasn't going to happen. Now, where are you headed?"

I took a silent breath and leaned against the elevator wall, staring down at my shoes. "To my uncle's office."

"Ninth floor, next stop." He turned and faced the door. "It's 909, and for the future, if you give me classified information, just let me know, and I'll lock my lips and throw away the key."

"Sorry I was such a grump," I told him. "Please accept my apology."

"Absolutely, kiddo," he said gently. "Now we both know the rules."

At floor nine, he opened the door with an encouraging nod.

Steeling my nerves, I proceeded to stomp down the hall to my Uncle Bernie's office. My rage returned; only this time, it was directed at the right person. I couldn't wait to tell Bernie to stay out of my life. Of course, not in those exact words. As I stood outside the big wooden door, I tried to think of another way to say it. Firm but not rude, bold but not brash, smart but not smart-alecky.

I stood there, ready to knock. The fact of the matter was I had no idea what I was going to say. I had never actually called out an adult before. I'd never had any reason to.

LIKE MY MOM, LAST time I had seen Uncle Bernie was when he had crashed Jeff's bar mitzvah. The celebration was at the Plaza Hotel. Janny hadn't invited him—her only brother, our only uncle—but she had invited every single other relative (some Jeff and I hadn't even known existed). One of them must have leaked it. So Bernie strolled in and kissed Janny hello as if he had been at the top of the guest list. I'll never forget the look of distaste in her eyes.

The ballroom was packed with boring, cheek-pinching grown-ups as well as Jeff's friends, who looked at me as if I was some sort of microbe. With nothing better to do, I sat down at the piano when the band took a break. I was just noodling around, not really playing a song, when I heard a gravelly voice behind me.

"Hey, Justice, baby, I didn't know you played piano. I'm your Uncle Bernie."

For an old guy, Uncle Bernie wasn't bad-looking. His

dark hair was slicked back, and he had a Florida tan that set off his really white teeth. He wore a shiny gray suit with a white flower in the buttonhole of his lapel. He was picking his teeth with a gold toothpick, which I found both disgusting and weirdly hypnotic.

Without waiting for an invitation, he slid onto the seat next to me, almost nudging me off. "You taking lessons?"

I shook my head, embarrassed, "No, I play by ear. I don't read very well, but I like to write songs."

"Do you?" His eyes lit up. "Let me hear something."

It was the first time anyone had ever asked me to play something I'd written. My entire family was always yelling at me to keep it down—"it" meaning any note, no matter how soft, I struck on the piano at home. Maybe that's why I didn't hesitate. I played him what now seems like a really babyish song. Still, I was only ten, and I thought it was great. It was called "When You Smile" or something dumb like that. But he sat very still with a serious face, as if he were completely riveted.

When I was finished, he nodded.

"I'm in the music business," he told me. His voice had changed; he spoke quickly and evenly now, as if talking to a grown-up. "I publish songs and manage recording artists. I've done it for a very long time. Do you want to know what I think of your song?"

"I do," I answered, trying to keep my own voice from shaking. The piano bench turned to pins and needles. This was a first. An opinion about one of my songs. I held my breath.

"I think you should keep on writing. One day, when

you've finished college, if you're still writing songs, I'd like you to come and play them for me. I think you have talent."

Before I had a chance to ask him anything else, the band members began to take the stage. He stepped off, and I lost him in the crowd. He must have left right after that, because I couldn't find him anywhere, even though I spent the rest of the night searching.

On the way home in the taxi, I asked Janny about him. She clammed up, muttering that it was rude to attend an event you weren't invited to, and Bernie was not someone she wanted me asking about or associating with. Jeff nudged me with his elbow, warning me to shut up.

That night, after our parents had gone to bed, I asked my brother what he knew.

"Uncle Bernie is Kosher Nostra," he whispered behind his closed bedroom door. "That's what they call the Jewish mob. He's got some kind of bad gambling habit, so he's always selling his recording companies to pay off the bookies, but he never sells his publishing companies 'cause he loves songs."

None of that made much sense to me. Why would Janny care if her brother gambled? Jules played poker with his friends. "Did you know he was at your bar mitzvah?" I asked.

Jeff grinned. "Yeah, he gave me an envelope stuffed with money. When Mom counted it, it was one thousand eight hundred dollars."

I frowned. "That's a weird number. Why not thirteen hundred for your bar mitzvah?"

"Dad told me when you give money gifts, they should be in multiples of eighteen, 'cause that's a lucky number in Jewish numerology. Most people give fifty-four or a hundred and eight, but Mom says Bernie likes to give big gifts just to show off."

And that was all I was able to find out about my Uncle Bernie.

NOW I STOOD OUTSIDE of Uncle Bernie's office door, nervously biting my cheek, furious at him for helping me get the job I wanted—which I never would have gotten without him. Nothing made sense. I didn't know if I was angry or grateful. Maybe I was both. I felt too mixed up to think straight.

Still at a loss as to how I was going to handle this, I stepped inside.

The secretary's desk was empty. She must have gone to lunch, so I made my way down a hall lined with gold records to Uncle Bernie's office.

The door was open. He was seated at a desk even bigger than Bobby's, almost as if he were waiting for me. He looked exactly the way he did at the bar mitzvah, tan and slick. The only difference was that his suit was navy with pinstripes. He was leaning back in a big leather chair, with his shiny patent shoes propped up on his desk, a huge grin on his face.

"Justice, baby!" he exclaimed. He checked his big gold watch and flashed his pearly whites. "You just made it. I gave Nick eight to five you'd be here by one thirteen."

CHAPTER SEVEN

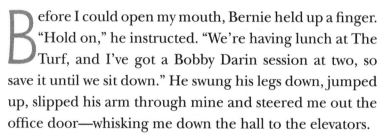

efore I could open my mouth, Bernie held up a finger. "Hold on," he instructed. "We're having lunch at The Turf, and I've got a Bobby Darin session at two, so save it until we sit down." He swung his legs down, jumped up, slipped his arm through mine and steered me out the office door—whisking me down the hall to the elevators.

He didn't even need to ring. The door opened as if by magic, and Nick welcomed us in.

"I'll let you have your say," Bernie promised as we rode down to the lobby. "Just wait until we're at our table."

I figured there wasn't much point in arguing. Besides, I could use the time to formulate my thoughts. Unfortunately the force of Uncle Bernie's personality wiped my mind clear. He was bigger than life. He was the Wizard of the Oz of the Brill Building.

THE TURF OCCUPIED PART of the lobby level. There were tables where diners could get Surf and Turf (lobster and steak), and a bar where, for fifty cents, you could sit on a stool and get roast beef on a bun. I noticed there were a lot of deferential smiles and nods toward Bernie from both tables and barstools. I also noticed we bypassed a line of people waiting to be seated. A corner table by the window was ours.

A waiter scurried over immediately and placed a cocktail in front of my uncle. I opened the towering menu, but Bernie didn't bother. He ordered the most expensive lunch for each of us—The Turf Special—without even asking me what I wanted. Then he leaned back, unfurled his napkin, and took a sip of his drink.

I shoved my menu into the waiter's hands. "Uncle Bernie—"

"Justice," he interrupted, "I'll bet you a nickel this is more or less what you were planning to say to me . . ."

"I don't want to bet—"

"It's just a nickel, Justice, baby. Don't give me a hard time, okay?"

I slumped back in my chair.

He took a sip of his drink and cleared his throat. At least he didn't try to imitate my voice. "'Uncle Bernie, I know you thought you were doing something nice when you stepped in and got me the job at Good Music, but it really upset me. I wanted to get that job on my own. I don't want or need anyone's help, especially yours.'"

I started to speak. Up came that finger again.

"'My mother says you're the black sheep of the family, and I should have nothing to do with you. So I wanted to let you know how I feel, because after this lunch I never want to see you again.'" He paused and took another sip. "That's pretty much it, right?"

I nodded sheepishly.

"So pay up," he said.

I laughed in spite of myself as I dug into my purse and dropped a nickel in the middle of the white tablecloth. A moment later, the waiter slid our lunch plates in front of us.

"If you knew I didn't want your help, why did you help me?" I asked him.

Bernie picked up his silverware and leaned over his plate. "Because if you do have talent, I want you to have the chance to find that out, and a job at Good Music is the way to do it. It's the best songwriting school you can go to."

I glanced around the restaurant. I wondered how many other people here were aspiring songwriters. "When Bobby didn't like my songs, I figured I didn't have any talent at all," I admitted.

"You have a lot to learn, Justice, baby. Lesson one: Bobby isn't always right. No one is. I'm only right about talent ninety percent of the time, and that's a damn good percentage." He flashed his irresistible, twinkly white smile and leaned in closer, palming the nickel. "As you can see, I take betting very seriously." His face grew serious as he leaned back. "I think you've got it, JJ. I saw it in your eyes and heard it in that little song you played me at your brother's bar mitzvah. I got the same feeling in my stomach as I did the first time I heard Carole King sing and play. She was fifteen. Now she's writing hit songs for everyone you can think of. I couldn't let you give up because one person discouraged you. I just couldn't."

My heart swelled. I wasn't sure what to make of this uncle who'd just conned me out of a nickel. On the other hand, I had never, ever received this much encouragement and understanding from *anyone*. Was it possible Uncle Bernie saw me in a way that no one in my family ever had? In spite of the warmth, I felt scared. Now I not only had to prove to my family that they were wrong about me, I also had to prove to Bernie that he was right.

"I should have come to your office to thank you," I said. "Can we make-believe I did that?"

He smiled, downed his drink, and motioned to the waiter for another. "Justice, baby, you and me should never make-believe about anything. I've got four ex-wives and a bunch of grown kids I don't get along with, and my problems always began with me not being honest with them. I don't want to make the same mistake with you."

I leaned across the expanse of tablecloth. "Then tell me honestly: are you the bad guy my mom thinks you are?"

Bernie heaved a weary sigh. "Some people would say I am." He started in on his lunch. "I've done some bad things in my time, but I don't think of myself that way. What I am is a guy who loves songs and this nutty business, who's sometimes done stuff he's not proud of." He met my gaze. "Is there anyone who *hasn't* done stuff they're not proud of?"

Before I could answer, a feminine voice cut in: "Sweetie, I knew you'd go nuts when you realized you forgot this."

I found myself staring up at one of the tallest and most beautiful women I had ever seen in my life. My jaw went slack. She was at least six feet in heels, with skin like porcelain and dark red hair that tumbled in waves around her shoulders. She looked like a younger version of Suzy Parker, the fashion model. Around her neck she wore a diamond grace note on a platinum chain. In her hand she clutched a small gold cylinder.

"Marla, baby, you're the best," Bernie murmured, taking the cylinder from her. With his free hand he pulled over an empty chair from a nearby table, and Marla deposited her beautiful self in it. "Justice, this is my wife, Marla."

Wife? I had thought she might be one of his grown kids. Uncle Bernie was five years older than my mom, so that made him forty-eight. She looked twenty-four, tops.

"I've heard all about you, honey," Marla said to me. She was one of those people who looked directly into your eyes and managed to smile and talk at the same time—like a Miss America. "Bernard thinks you're going to be a great songwriter some day."

"I . . . uh . . . um . . . hope he's right," I stammered as Bernie unscrewed the gold capsule, removed a gold toothpick and engaged in some serious dental house cleaning—just like he'd done at Jeff's bar mitzvah.

"Uncle Bernie," I stage-whispered, "don't you know that is considered very rude?"

Bernie laughed so loudly that he drew a few stares. "From one rebel to another, JJ. That's why I love to do it."

Marla rolled her gorgeous hazel eyes. "If you can put up with your uncle's bad manners, I'd love you to come for dinner at our place," she said warmly. "Pick an evening and let Bernie know."

"I will. I definitely will." I stared down at my plate, grinning foolishly, not hungry in the least.

The rest of the lunch was a blur. I walked out of the restaurant floating on air. I was on the high of someone who had found a believer. My uncle had managed to give me more confidence in forty minutes than the rest of my family had in an entire lifetime.

CHAPTER EIGHT

O ut in the real world, it seemed that something horrible was happening every day. George Wallace, the
governor of Alabama, stood on the steps of the state
university to stop two Negro students from registering.
It wasn't until President Kennedy called in the National
Guard that Governor Wallace was forced to step aside
and let them in. The next day, Medgar Evers, one of the
leaders of the NAACP, was shot and killed outside his
house in Mississippi. It felt as if the country were losing
its mind. I began to tune out my parents' discussions of
the headlines at breakfast. Everything was so depressing.
But a part of me worried about those students in Alabama.
I wondered if could ever stand up for what I believed in
with that much courage.

Good Music wasn't just a haven where I could forget
about all the chaos beyond the Brill Building. It was also
a place where nobody seemed to think that skin color
was anything to get upset about. Janny and Jules were

self-proclaimed "Civil Libertarians" and fierce advocates for Negro rights, but they didn't have any close colored friends. Neither did Jeff. Neither did I. Radio was still divided between the rhythm and blues stations—the ones that played Wilson Pickett—and the white stations, the ones that were starting to play more surf stuff now that summer was here, like Jan and Dean and The Beach Boys.

But music was beginning to break down racial barriers on the airwaves. And everyone at Good Music could feel it.

WHEN I WASN'T COPYING or filing while listening to my Sony transistor radio, I ran errands for the songwriters. I always took a few minutes to stand outside their cubicle doors, eavesdropping before I brought in their coffee. I wanted to hear their writing process. Bernie was absolutely right; I had a lot to learn. A whole lot of new curse words, for one thing. I found out that lots of romantic love songs were born in a not-so-romantic atmosphere. I also picked up some chord changes and suspensions I had never dreamed of, much less tried.

My second week on the job, Rona told me I could even borrow demos overnight if I returned them the next day. Demos were short for demonstration records and that's exactly what they were. The songwriters recorded basic versions of their songs to demonstrate what they hoped the final recording would sound like. They wanted their 12-inch vinyl demos to be the basis of the more elaborate final record. Bobby played these demos for singers, record producers, and record companies to show his writers' work. They were his ultimate sales tool.

Good Music was famous for its great demos. The

songwriters were given a small allowance to record them. Anything over the budget came out of their own pockets. So one of them usually sang and played piano—and hired a guitarist, bassist, and drummer from a regular crew of professional demo musicians.

Now that I had the chance to listen to and learn from them in my very own bedroom, I rarely slept more than four hours a night.

Every bleary morning I would see Green Eyes in the elevator. We were both loaded down with folders. Unfortunately, my folders didn't seem to make me any more attractive to him. He was in his own world and wanted to keep it that way. Those eyes were dazzling but distant. And sad somehow. But that wasn't my problem. I wasn't here to meet a boy. I was here to learn how to be a songwriter.

MY SECOND WEDNESDAY ON the job, Bobby began a practice that would become a weekly ritual. He'd stick his head in the copy room and ask, "Got anything, JJ, babe?"

Translation: *Do you have a song to play for me?*

On Wednesdays, publishers would call *Cashbox* and *Billboard*, the trade papers, to find out the chart numbers for the following week. It was the day when Bobby's song lust was at its peak. Maybe because it was the day he learned whether his writers' songs went up or down on the Top 100 chart. Since writers and publishers shared the royalties that the records earned, his business was literally going up and down with them.

On that day I could tell by everyone's face what kind of news they had gotten that week. Good Music was its own world within the world of the Brill Building. The songwriters worked with, played with, gossiped with, flirted with, and romanced one other. It was like a musical soap opera, with secrets, scandals, and intrigue. A smoky soap opera. Everyone smoked their brains out. I reeked of cigarettes so much that I had to convince my parents I hadn't taken up the habit myself. But other than blowing smoke at me, the writers didn't acknowledge my existence. They were all a few years older, so I sort of understood. But it made me angry, too, which in turn made me more determined to earn their respect by writing a song of my own.

On Wednesdays, Bobby also posted a list of who was looking for songs to record. I pretended I was a real staff writer and tried to write for someone on the list, but nothing I came up with sounded half as good as what I was hearing from the Good Music songwriters. I began to stay late so I could write on what I called the "magic pianos," the uprights in the cubicles where the real writers wrote their hits. The office was so quiet at night, I could feel the creativity in the walls. None of it had yet seeped into my fingers, but I knew if I was going to write, that was the place to do it. Janny and Jules gave me permission to stay late, as long I came home no later than eleven. I think they were both relieved that I wasn't hammering on the keyboard in the living room. And I made sure to always make it home on time so they wouldn't have an excuse to forbid the late hours.

THE FRIDAY AFTER BOBBY first poked his head into my cubicle, I accepted Marla's invitation to dinner with her and Bernie.

They didn't live far from the Brill Building, so I was able to walk there. I planned to come back and try to write after we ate. Of course, I didn't say a word about the dinner plans to my mother. She had no idea I'd even *seen* Bernie. As far as the Green family was concerned, I hadn't had any direct contact with my no-goodnik uncle since Jeff's bar mitzvah. I wanted to keep it that way.

Bernie and Marla's apartment was even more spacious and music-biz fabulous than I'd imagined, the walls lined with expensive art and gold records. When a singer or songwriter under Bernie's management went gold for sales of half a million by the record company, it seemed that Bernie somehow managed to get a gold record, too— just like he was the recording artist. He was very good at his job and clearly had a ferocious sense of entitlement.

Best of all was the Steinway Grand in the living room. It was the most beautiful piano I'd ever seen, polished mahogany, and arranged on it were silver framed photos of Bernie with every music star you could imagine—from Elvis Presley to Frank Sinatra.

By the time we sat down to dinner, I was buzzing. They did most of the talking, but I was happy to listen. I found out that they had met in Las Vegas, where Marla was a showgirl—in other words, "someone who just walked around the stage looking beautiful in a skimpy costume with a huge headdress." It had been love at first sight for both of them, Marla claimed. The two of them had gotten married at the Little White Wedding Chapel after knowing each other for less than a week. Three years later they still acted like playful newlyweds.

After dessert, Bernie insisted on giving me a pile of records he wanted me to study. Like Bobby, he wanted me to get in tune with what was popular: Bobby Vinton, Bobby Rydell, and groups like The Drifters and The Shirelles.

"Listen, Justice, baby," he told me, gripping my shoulders, "what I want you to always remember is that it all begins with the song. Without the song, there's nothing for the singer to sing, nothing for the record company to release, and nothing for the public to fall in love with. If you're really one of the lucky ones blessed with the gift to create music, you've got to stick with it, not just for yourself but for the rest of the world."

I swallowed hard. "I will, I promise. But you have to promise that you'll only help me with advice. I want to succeed or fail on my own. Do you promise?"

"He promises," Marla said sweetly. She gently pried my uncle away and added in a mock-menacing tone, "Don't you, Bernie?"

Uncle Bernie laughed, throwing up his hands in defeat. "I'm outnumbered."

"You just tell me if he doesn't behave, JJ," Marla whispered with a wink. "I have ways of getting him back in line."

For the first time in my life, I hated to leave a "family" event. They were like champagne, and the Greens were like tap water. But they also understood that I had work to do. They both insisted on walking with me right up to the Brill Building elevator where they turned me over to Nick.

a HaLF HOUr LaTer, alone at an upright, the magic still hadn't transferred itself to my fingers. It wasn't easy to get back into writing mode. I was stuffed and sleepy, but I had a deadline. I'd started fooling around with some of those new chord progressions floating around the office, experimenting with a melody that had been flitting through my brain that wasn't half bad.

I was getting tired, though. I finally lifted my fingers, arched my back, and stretched.

At first I thought someone had turned on a radio. But the radio never plays a solo vocal with no backing. Besides, the sound was too rich and too real. It was live. I knew that song. I knew that soulful aching sound. It was a voice from long ago, somehow here with me right now, right outside my door. The song was "Good Love Gone Bad," a hit in the late forties or early fifties, right around the time when Billie Holiday and Sarah Vaughan were putting out hit singles.

I jumped up and peeked out the door. The only person out there was the cleaning woman. Her back was toward me. She sang as she emptied the wastepaper baskets and wiped off the desks in the big room, oblivious to everything but the glorious music she was making. I left the door halfway open and slid onto the piano bench again. My hands automatically found the chords to support the melody and the voice, and we became one—one sound, one being, in service of the song. The voice grew louder. I could tell she was moving closer to my cubicle. I turned just as the door swung all the way open.

"It can't be," I gasped, not believing my eyes. "It's you!"

CHAPTER NINE

"Sweet" Dulcie Brown was a soul/jazz/pop singer from the days before rock and roll took over the airwaves. Nobody else my age would have known who she was, but I did. I'd read all about her in a book called *The Blues Is a Woman*, which chronicled the lives of great soul singers from Ma Rainey and Bessie Smith to Dinah Washington and the woman who was standing in front of me now. The book described everything they had overcome from poverty-ridden childhoods to bad adult relationships. Like so many before her, Dulcie had once been stunningly gorgeous, with a number-one song and a great career ahead of her—and then like so many, she had burned out in a blaze of drugs and personal disasters.

Now she was in the doorway, singing in that voice that was almost too beautiful to bear. It was filled with such obvious pain that I wondered how one person could have suffered so much and found a way to put all those feelings into her art. She kept singing, and my hands fell back to the keys. Then she moved close to the piano, and by the time we hit the last chorus, she was standing next to me.

I looked up at her. Our eyes locked. When we hit the final chord together, we couldn't help but smile at each other.

She was a few pounds heavier than in her glory days, but she'd been too thin back then. So, now she looked perfect. She still had cheekbones that could cut glass. Her wide-set hazel eyes had some wrinkles at the corners, but they just added to the sweetness of her smile. Even in jeans and a work shirt, she was still a knockout.

"You got a feel for that keyboard, girl," she said. "Who taught you to play like that?"

My face flushed. "I think you did."

"What do you mean?"

"I was inspired by the way you sang that song. I have a copy of your record at home. I've played it a million times."

"But you were a baby when that record came out. How'd you ever get a copy?"

"I saved up for it," I told her. "And bought it at the Colony."

"That sure is a compliment," Dulcie breathed. "My sweet Lord. What's your name, honey?"

"JJ Green, Miss Brown," I answered.

"My name's Dulcie to you. Are you a writer here?"

"I hope to be, but right now I'm just an assistant."

She sat down on the piano bench next to me. "Will you play me something you've written?"

I hesitated, staring at the keys. "I would, but I don't really like anything I've written so far."

"How about what you were just working on? I heard it out there. That didn't sound so bad to me."

"Really?"

"Really." She nodded.

I began to play the melody I had just found, becoming more confident as I went along. I'd been following Bobby's orders, listening to the radio, checking out the Top Forty whenever I could. Sitting here now, I suddenly realized that I had been absorbing pop, rock and roll, and rhythm and blues without even knowing it. Some of that world seemed to be seeping into my own writing. My new melody had the ache of Ray Charles's "I Can't Stop Loving You," with a bassline that added tension until it exploded into a simple repetitive chorus. It was only a melody without words. Still, I was pretty sure it had what Bobby called a hook, that musical phrase you hear once and want to hear again until you can't get it out of your head.

"Play it again, JJ, honey," Dulcie encouraged.

The second time around, she began to hum along, picking up the tempo a bit, changing the syncopation of my bass riff. The way she sang turned my melodic phrases slightly—in a good way. They actually sounded more radio friendly. I changed what I was playing to match her, and I couldn't help but smile. How could this feel so good? It seemed strange that someone whose frame of reference was a decade past could make my melody sound so con-temporary. We ran through it a few more times until I had it all in my fingers.

"You should be my co-writer," I blurted out.

Dulcie waved her hand and stood. "Hell no, girl. It's

yours. I'm just showing you what you got in there. Now you have to find the right words, and I have to get back to work."

I frowned. "But you—"

"Hush now," she whispered, cutting me off. "You made my day by knowing my song." She smiled, her eyes distant, and absently ran a finger over a delicate gold chain around her neck. Hanging from it was a musical grace note, like Marla's diamond one. Only this one seemed to be made out of something I could actually save up for.

"I love your necklace," I murmured. "Where'd you get it?"

"A very good friend gave it to me, so I never take it off." She lowered her voice like we were old girlfriends. "I'll ask him where he got it. Now I have to get back to my job."

"Will I see you again?" I askcd.

Dulcie's smile widened. "I'll be here, girl, so you work on that song." With a wave she was out the door.

I checked my watch. It was 10:15. I had to be heading home.

A few minutes later, when I hurried out of the office, Dulcie was already gone. It was weird. We'd just met, barely knew each other, and yet I felt she knew me better than anyone else at Good Music. And I wanted to know her. Now I had more than one reason for working late.

CHAPTER TEN

I pretended I had cramps on Sunday night so I could stay home and work on my melody when the family went out for dinner together. I hated to pull that excuse—it was so junior high school—but it always worked. Anyway, I needed time alone, and that was the only way to get it.

In my pajamas, with almost three hours to myself, I polished the verses and chorus and even got a concept for a bridge: that third but crucial section of the song featuring a different melody than the verse or chorus. I didn't even try to think of a lyric idea yet.

That part of it scared me to death. Dulcie would be waiting to hear it. How could any of my words live up to the melody she helped me write?

THE NEXT MORNING I spotted Mr. GE at the elevator. I didn't even glance his way. I had given up trying to get his attention. We were both loaded down with folders. Mine were stuffed with lead sheets I'd been studying and demos I'd borrowed. His were no doubt filled with all the phone numbers of girls he thought were cute and planned to call, with mine conspicuously absent.

We were the first ones in the elevator. I stood in the center, giving him plenty of room to stay far away from me.

"Look at you two workaholics," commented Nick. "You kids were made for each other."

My eyes narrowed to slits. I shushed him. As the crowd surged into the car, someone bumped into me. I was pushed into Green Eyes so hard that we both dropped our folders.

Blood rushed to my face. Everything spilled out onto the elevator floor. I gasped apologies as the other passengers stooped to help us pick up our stuff, handing back the scattered papers and records. When we reached seven, GE pushed his way out without so much as a backward glance, just a terse thank-you.

As soon as I made it into Good Music, I found an empty songwriting cubicle and tried to organize all the lead sheets and demos. Everything of mine was there.

But so was something that didn't belong to me.

It was at the bottom of the pile: a piece of legal pad paper. Lyrics, clearly. But the words were scrawled all over the page as if the person who'd written them couldn't write fast enough.

> *I have to go where my heart takes me*
> *And believe what I believe.*
> *And I gotta trust even if that trust breaks me,*
> *I'm not gonna take my heart off my sleeve.*

Our tomorrows are dreams we may never see
Still I loved you with all the love I had in me.

And I'm glad I did, though it may hurt me now.
I loved you as long as our time would allow.
Yes, I'm glad I did, and I treasure what we had
With all we went through I was blessed to love you
Through the good times and the bad
I'm glad . . . so glad I did.

I read it again. Then a third time. *Wow*, was all I could think. Who was this song about? It had to belong to Green Eyes, but I had no idea if he had written it.

I put the lyrics on the piano, shut the door and began fitting some of the words to my melody. The title and some of the chorus fit perfectly. I made some melodic changes to accommodate the words. The changes actually made the melody better. The verses didn't match my verse, yet somehow I knew it could be a song. The emotion in the music and words meshed as if they had been written together.

It seemed too good to be true. Things like this didn't normally happen to me. I was more likely to find someone's laundry list. I had a feeling Green Eyes would be pissed off if he knew what I'd done. It was a bit nervy.

There was a knock on the door. Rona opened up. "There you are," she announced. "I've been looking all over for you."

"Sorry, I lost track of time."

"Come on, JJ, a whole bunch of new demos and lead sheets have to be filed."

I followed her and plunged back into the drone work that only last week had excited me. This week it was an endless chore. I couldn't wait to get back to my melody.

At lunchtime, there was a knock on the door of my little file and copy room. When I opened it, I was surprised to see Bernie standing there holding *Cashbox* and *Billboard*. "These are for you, a present from me. You free for lunch?"

How could I refuse?

AND SO WE BEGAN what was to become our regular weekly lunch-date-and-music-business-education session. Every Monday, either at The Turf or Jack Dempsey's Restaurant, the other Brill Building hot spot. Dempsey's was strictly for the rich publisher/manager crowd, so Bernie favored it. It was really expensive. Roast beef and a baked potato cost $5.75. Even Bobby's writers couldn't afford that. But that was okay, because it meant that it was unlikely anyone would spot us together.

"So, Justice, baby," he'd always begin. "This is important . . ."

And then he'd hold forth on some topic like music publishing, or copyright, or royalties—both mechanical and performance—or performing rights organizations like BMI and ASCAP. After that he'd move on to record companies, synch royalties, sheet music, attorneys, managers or record producers. It seemed that the List of Important Things went on forever, and so did Uncle Bernie's knowledge. I knew I'd never remember everything he was telling me. But some of it had to stick. Most of all, I knew I was really lucky to have him in my life.

Still, I couldn't wait to get back to my empty songwriting cubicle.

LATER THAT AFTERNOON, RONA had me checking demo invoices to be sure that the writers weren't spending more than fifty dollars a demo. If they did, it got charged back against them. That explained the heated discussions among the writing teams about whether a song needed a sax or horns. Now I couldn't help but put myself in the mix. I felt a prickle of excitement. I knew when I was ready to record my demo, I'd come in under fifty bucks.

Before I knew it, it was six o'clock. I called home to say I was feeling much better, actually well enough to stay and work. My mom sounded relieved that I had made a rapid recovery and gave me her blessing.

I felt a little guilty for getting around her so easily, but when I thought about seeing Dulcie, the guilt disappeared.

I left the door open a crack. Sure enough, at eight o'clock, there was a gentle knock.

"I heard you playin' for a while now," she told me. "I didn't want to break your flow." She had a dust rag in one hand. She was wearing the same blouse and jeans she'd worn on Friday—the same necklace, too.

"Would you come in and listen?" I asked her. "I've even got some words."

"Sure thing." She sat down beside me on the piano bench. I was really nervous to sing the lyrics for her. I was worried as to whether she would like it and even more worried that my songwriter singing voice wouldn't do the words justice. I had crafted the chorus to the words, but the verses still had empty lines. I don't know why, but I knew she would understand it anyway—and she did.

When I was done, I turned to her.

"This is soulful, girl," she told me. "Play that chorus again for me, will you?"

Seconds after my fingers hit the keys, she wrapped her beautiful voice around the words. Suddenly they had depth. And tenderness. They really meant something now.

She laid a hand over mine, interrupting my playing. "You write these words, baby? They are deep."

"I'm not sure who wrote them," I told her, a little embarrassed. "I kind of found them."

"Found them?" She arched an eyebrow.

"It was, well . . . it was in the elevator. I dropped a bunch of papers, and so did some guy. Everything got all mixed up, and I ended up with—"

"With these lyrics? You gotta find out who wrote them," Dulcie interrupted firmly. "You gotta ask that person if they'll let you set their words to music. You can't just go and do it without permission."

I bit my lip, then nodded quickly. "I know, I know. I just got so excited about how the words fit that I got carried away. Don't worry, I know where to go to find out."

She patted my shoulder. "Get that squared away, 'cause you're on the right track with this, JJ, girl. I got a good feeling."

I sighed, staring at the keyboard. "I don't think Bobby's gonna like it. He only likes really happy songs."

"My grandma wouldn't like it either," Dulcie stated

seriously. Then, seeing the look on my face, she burst out laughing. "She dead, baby girl. She ain't got no opinions."

I couldn't help but burst out laughing, too. She opened her arms. I hugged her like an old friend, closing my eyes, enjoying the warmth of her embrace. I wished I could have shared this kind of moment with Janny. It was so natural, so spontaneous.

"I gotta get back to work," Dulcie reminded both of us, standing up. "Don't let that lyric get away."

"I won't," I said. "I promise."

"I'll check in with you." She picked up her dust cloth and heading for the door. "Gotta make sure you nail down those words."

As soon as the door closed, I got a scary feeling in the pit of my stomach. I was dreading facing Mr. Green Eyes. I began to wonder if it was possible to ignore someone who was talking directly to you. I had a feeling I'd find out.

CHAPTER ELEVEN

The next morning, I ducked out of Rona's sight at 10:25. It was post-morning rush hour; pre-first coffee run. Elevator traffic would be light. I got doubly lucky. When I buzzed for the elevator, Nick opened the door, and the car was empty.

"I need info," I told him.

"Come into my office," he replied with a courtly gesture. I stepped in, and he closed the elevator door. "Whaddya need?"

"Do you know who the guy with the green eyes and the folders is? The one who dropped his stuff with me?"

"I don't know who he is, but I know where he is, which is almost as good," Nick replied. "You gonna ask him for a date?"

"No, I am not," I stated firmly. "I'm just returning something of his, so stop trying to be a matchmaker, please. Just tell me where he is."

Nick smirked. "The number is seven seventeen. He's

working out of George Silver's office. Which is kinda strange."

"Strange how?" I asked.

Nick shrugged. "George was a manager and publisher bigwig like your uncle, but he died about a month ago. Since then this kid's been coming in every day, spending all day at George's office. He leaves at about seven with a big stack of files."

I turned this information over in my head. I wasn't sure what to make of it. Nick was right; it *was* strange. "I gotta get back to the office," I said. "But I'll be back at six P.M. hoping for an express to seven."

"It's only one floor down. I think I can arrange an express." Nick grinned as he pulled the elevator door open. "See ya later, kiddo."

I MaDe IT BaCK before Rona even knew I was gone. The minutes dragged like hours for the rest of the day. All I could think about was finding some new way to make a fool of myself in front of Green Eyes. There was the tripping-over-my-own-feet scenario, the stammering and stuttering scenario and best of all, the staring-through-me-as-if-I-weren't-there scenario. By the time the last Good Music writer had left, and six o'clock had arrived, I was a nervous wreck. I had no idea what I was going to say.

When Nick deposited me on the seventh floor, I knew I had to pull myself together. *All he can tell me is no,* I told myself. *No big deal.*

But it was a big deal. Dulcie Brown was expecting me to deliver those lyrics.

Seven seventeen was almost opposite the elevator. The sign on the door read GEORGE SILVER MUSIC. I opened it without knocking. There was no reception area, just a large room that was a real mess. Folders and papers were piled everywhere: on the couch, chairs and tabletops. The walls were covered with photographs, BMI awards, and gold records. There were more stacked in cartons on the floor. In a corner was an upright piano with piles of sheet music and lead sheets on top of it. And seated at a huge desk in front of the window was Green Eyes himself, totally engrossed in a file.

I coughed a fake cough to let him know that I'd entered. He looked up. I knew it was impossible, but it seemed his eyes had gotten greener. Maybe it was the pale green shirt he was wearing that brought out those cat eyes of his. They contrasted perfectly with his olive skin and black curly hair. He was ridiculously handsome. So much so that all my scenarios chased one another through my mind.

"Yes," he said, as if he had never seen me before. "Can I help you?"

"I'm the girl from the elevator," I said, regaining my composure. "We dropped our folders. I think someone accidentally returned something of yours to me." I handed him the paper with the words on it.

He gave it a quick scan. "Oh, yeah," he said. "This is mine. Thanks." He went right back to whatever he was doing. He didn't even offer a smile.

I stood there for a moment and fake-coughed again. "Look, I don't mean to be pushy. But I'm working at Good

Music, and those words and a melody I wrote are kind of
made for each other. Did you write them?"

"Yeah," he said, looking up.

"Well, what I'm getting at is that I'd really like to play
what I have for you. I set your first verse and chorus."

He stood, even though he didn't look particularly happy
about making the effort. "Sure, play me what you've got,"
he answered. "Sorry if I seem kind of distracted. There's a
lot of work to be done here." Seeing my questioning look,
he went on, waving around at the mess. "This was my dad's
office. He was sick, and he wasn't able to come in for a
long time. He passed away recently. So I've been cleaning
things up and putting them in order."

"Oh, I'm really sorry." I backed toward the door. "If this
is a bad time . . ."

"No, I apologize," he interrupted. "I'm annoyed at
myself for dropping what you found. I was bringing it
in to the office to try to write a melody on my dad's
funky piano. I'm not much of a melody writer, though."
He moved around to the front of the desk, still holding
the lyrics, and extended his hand. "I'm Luke Silver," he
said.

"JJ Green," I replied, shaking his hand—which felt
impersonal, warm, and strangely familiar, as if all of those
qualities could even go together. "I'm really sorry about
your dad."

"Thanks. It was a long time coming." Luke glanced at
the piano. "Come on, have a seat. It'll be good for me to
get my mind off what I'm doing here for a few minutes."

I sat, and he settled on the bench next to me. I was

conscious of his closeness, but he didn't seem to notice. I focused and played him what I had, trying to bring some of Dulcie's passion for the words to my performance. But my vocals were amateur compared to hers. In the spots where I didn't have enough words I just sang *la-las*. By the time I finished, I felt like a jerk. I couldn't even look at him.

"That's kind of amazing," he said softly.

I jerked around, meeting his eyes. "Really?"

He nodded. "Play it again. A few more times."

As I started in again, he grabbed a pen from the top of the piano and jotted notes. By the third time around, he had produced another paper with a second verse. We went over that a few times. Then he began to sing what he'd added, looking at me with a questioning look whenever he tweaked my melody in the slightest. His voice wasn't great, but it was in tune. I just nodded. What he was doing made my melody even better.

"I'm not usually this fast, but it's all been in my head for a long time," he said with a fleeting grin, almost as if he were talking to himself.

"I've got the bridge," I told him. "Can you write to it?"

I played it for him, and he scribbled away without a word.

And I'll be proud for as long as I live
That I gave someone everything I had to give

We went over it until it felt comfortable. The words and music began to feel like they had been born at the same moment. When I sang it through the last time, he joined me in harmony on the final chorus.

And I'm glad I did, though it may hurt me now.
I loved you as long as our time would allow.
Yes, I'm glad I did, and I treasure what we had
With all we went through I was blessed to love you
Through the good times and the bad
I'm glad . . . so glad I did.

The last chord died away. We looked into each other's eyes.

"I think we have a song," I said. I was trying not to smile like a fool, but it was impossible. I tried to keep my voice businesslike. "What do you think?"

"I think we nailed it." His eyes glittered. It was the first time I'd seen him look really alive.

"So if it's okay with you, I'd like to cut a demo," I said.

"Sure. You planning to do the vocal?"

I almost laughed. "No! Not on this. I'm just a songwriter-type singer. I have a very unlikely but very good vocalist I'd like to use. Have you ever heard of Sweet Dulcie Brown?"

His eyes widened. "Heard of her? My dad and his ex-partner used to manage Dulcie when I was little. How do you know her?"

"She's working as a custodian here in this building."

"Here in this building?" he echoed incredulously.

I nodded. "I met her last week when she was cleaning the office. She helped me shape the melody. When she sang some of it, I couldn't believe how good she sounded."

"I can't believe my dad never told me she worked here," he said, half to himself. "Maybe he didn't know. Or maybe she started after he got sick. She should have had a great career according to him. She just had a bad run-in with drugs, and after a while he and his partner, Bernie Rubin, had to drop her."

I almost fell off the piano bench. "Bernie Rubin?"

Luke nodded absently. "Yeah, he was my dad's partner years ago."

"Bernie's my uncle. That makes us kind of related . . . but not really," I added.

He smiled at that. A real honest-to-goodness smile. I'd made it happen. It was a first, and I hoped not a last.

"Listen, I gotta go," I told him. "Here's the thing: I'm working as an assistant and songwriter in training at Good Music. But I don't want to play this for Bobby just yet. I want to have the demo in my pocket and wait until just the right artist is coming up to record."

He nodded. "I get it. And you want Dulcie to sing lead."

"Yeah, I haven't asked her yet, but I plan to. I know it's a little crazy, so I can pay for the demo myself. I've got some birthday money saved."

"No way," Luke countered. "Co-writers share demo costs. How many musicians do you want to use?"

"Just bass, guitar, drums, and me on piano. It shouldn't be more than fifty bucks. I'd like to record at Dick Charles Studio Friday evening. Do you want to come?"

"I can't," Luke said, pulling two tens and a five out of his pocket and handing them to me. "I'm selling the apartment my dad and I lived in. There are potential buyers coming every night this week. But come by any time after you're done and play it for me. I really like what we did together today."

"Me, too," I said. "Thanks for letting me use your lyrics."

"Thank you for making it sound so good. This is my first song."

"It's my first collaboration," I admitted. I didn't want to leave, but I knew I had to get back to the office if I wanted to catch Dulcie. Still, I was dying to see him smile again. I turned before heading out the office door. "Could I ask you something personal?"

"I have a feeling that it doesn't matter what I say. You'll find a way to ask it," Luke answered, but his tone was good-natured.

"Well, my mom always taught me to ask if I wanted to know something. Did you write those lyrics about a girl in your life?"

"No," said Luke. "It wasn't about a girl."

"A boy?" I asked with bated breath.

His face lit up with that magical smile. "It wasn't about a boy either." He laughed. "And I'm not telling you any more than that today."

I'd seen it. I'd seen the smile. I could go now.

"Bye," I said.

"Bye, JJ." He sat down at the desk and buried his nose back in his father's files.

I floated out of the office and grinned as I pushed the elevator button. When Nick pulled open the door, I almost hugged him.

"So?" Nick asked. "Who is he?"

"George Silver's son and a very good songwriter," I replied. "And that's it for now."

I DASHED INTO THE office, dying to tell Dulcie everything and play her "I'm Glad I Did." The office was empty, though. Clean and empty. Tacked to the door of my adopted cubicle was a note.

I just know you got those words. Can't wait to hear the finished masterpiece.

Your friend,
Dulcie.

My friend Dulcie. My heart swelled. I folded the paper and put it in my pocket to save forever.

CHAPTER TWELVE

The next day would be a *woe is me* or *whoopee* Wednesday depending on the charts. As it turned out, it was both. A few Good Music songs took respectable jumps up the charts. That was the whoopee. The woe was that Bobby's pride and joy, a number-one record that had been riding in that slot for two weeks, fell. It really was seeing the glass half empty when you get depressed because your number one song is not number one anymore.

When he poked his head in the copy room for his weekly check-in, he was grumpier than usual.

"Got anything, JJ, babe?" he snapped.

"Workin' on it—"

He slammed the door. "Rona?" I heard him yell. "Why isn't she writing?"

"She is, Bobby," Rona responded in a soothing voice. "She's a perfectionist. Give her time. I've got Quincy Jones on the phone."

I could almost feel an imaginary rush of wind as I flew

out of Bobby's mind. Thanks to Rona, a list of songs for Quincy's recording artist, Leslie Gore, was flying in. I'd been all but forgotten. Rona was a pal. No doubt about it. The only other thing that got me through my drone day was thinking about hooking up with Dulcie after work.

WHEN THE LAST PERSON had finally left the office, and I had rehearsed the song at least ten times, I stared at my watch until I heard that gentle knock at the door.

"I thought I'd be hearing you singing," Dulcie said with a worried expression. "Don't tell me you didn't get the words."

"I won't tell you that," I answered, grinning.

"Then whatcha waiting for, girl?" she said, returning my smile. "Sing me that song."

By now I knew the lyrics by heart, so when she was seated beside me, I closed my eyes even though I had the words propped up on the piano. Then I sang my heart out. When I was done, Dulcie drew in a breath and let out a long sigh.

"*That* is a song. A soulful, soulful song," she said. "I could have used something like that back in my day. It's real special." She took my hands off the keys and folded them in hers. "You're going to have a beautiful career, baby girl."

She was looking at me with something I couldn't name, something I knew I had always wanted to see in my mother's eyes. I felt confused and sad and happy all at once. I took my hand back to wipe my eyelashes. "I think I'm allergic to compliments," I whispered huskily. "I'm all teary an' stuff."

"I know how it is," Dulcie half-whispered. "Now how

about you play it and let me sing to show you a few possibilities? You don't have to use anything I sing, but you can if you want to."

She riffed over the intro, just humming but setting up the emotion that was to come. Then while she was looking at the lyrics, she changed the opening line from *I have to go where my heart takes me/ And believe what I believe* to *I'm gonna go where my heart takes me/ Keep believin' what I believe.* Just by switching the words *have to* to *gonna* and changing the *and believe* to *keep believin'*, the song became more conversational, more powerful, more authentic. She sang through it, turning the melody in spots to make it more bluesy, occasionally replacing a word to make it more controversial. I was going crazy trying to remember everything she changed.

"Don't worry," Dulcie said, when she had sung it down. "I remember everything I did. If you like it, we can go over all of it until you have it all down."

And so we worked like that for the next hour. Lyrically and melodically, we took the song Luke and I had created and turned it into something better than I could have ever imagined. I learned as much from Dulcie Brown in that hour as I had from weeks of listening to the radio, eavesdropping outside the writers' room and immersing myself in the records Bernie had lent me. I also realized how much a great singer brought to a song. I drank in her performance. I think I absorbed some of her soul. When we were finally done, I turned to her.

"I have to ask you something," I said. "But please feel free to say no if you're not comfortable doing it. I'm recording the demo on Friday night at nine o'clock. Will you sing the vocal?"

Dulcie stood up. Even in her work clothes she was still so beautiful.

"I would be honored," she whispered. She leaned over. With her hands cradling my face, she kissed the top of my head. Then Sweet Dulcie Brown exited with her own head held high, looking as proud and fulfilled as if she were leaving the stage.

THURSDAY DAWNED HOT AND humid, but I bounded out of the apartment, ready to take on the day. I made it into the office early so I'd have time to play over "I'm Glad I Did" at least a hundred times. At eleven o'clock, I called Luke and told him I wanted to stop by for a few minutes at lunch to play him a few changes I'd made to the lyrics.

When I opened the door this time, his desk was much neater. Two sandwiches and two Cokes were set on paper-towel placemats.

He stood up. "Hope you haven't eaten. And that you like BLTs on whole wheat."

Of course I loved BLTs on whole wheat. If he'd gotten me peanut butter and pickle on pumpernickel, I would have loved that. The idea that he brought in lunch for me made my heart soar and my stomach rumble.

"Yes to both," I answered. "I'd really like to get the work part out of the way, though. I'll digest better if I know how you feel about the song now."

"Let's hear it," he replied as we both moved to the piano bench.

I played and sang with every bit of soul I could muster. I was no Dulcie Brown, but I was better than I had been when I last sang it for Luke.

When I was finished, he took a deep breath and shook his head. "I don't know what to say," he murmured. "It's so much better now. It's more real, more natural. Did you make these fixes?"

"No, Dulcie Brown did. When she sang it down, she made all these adjustments naturally."

"Maybe she should be our co-writer," Luke suggested. "She took it to another level."

I nodded eagerly. "I felt the same way, but she insists that she doesn't want a writing credit. She says she's just showing us what we have. And she's willing to sing on the demo."

"Damn, I wish I could be there."

"Me, too," I said. "I'm scared I'll screw it up somehow."

He rolled those green eyes. "If I thought that, I'd ask you to postpone it until I could be there. You know this song inside out. You'll be fine. Now let's eat, okay?"

"I guess," I mumbled, "but let me pay you for the sandwich."

"JJ, has anyone ever told you that you can be a pain?"

"Pretty much everyone," I confessed.

Only then did he smile for the first time since I'd walked in. I had to admit to myself, it was a big part of what I'd come for.

CHAPTER THIRTEEN

The next morning, I couldn't wait to see the "Artists Looking for Songs" list. If there was anyone there who could sing "I'm Glad I Did," I would finally be in the competition. And if someone recorded it, I would have accomplished my goal. I'd have proven Bernie right and Janny wrong. I'd be a real songwriter, and my family would have to recognize that.

My fantasies were off and running. This song would climb the charts. Luke and I would become a team professionally and romantically. We'd write every day and go to the writers' parties at Good Music. Bobby would love us. We'd be inside the magic circle . . .

The list was filled with girls groups like The Chiffons and The Ronettes. My heart sank. There wasn't a single person there who was right for our song. I was hoping to see Ray Charles's name. He had the vocal chops to handle it. But he wasn't looking for songs this week.

In the meantime, Rona took it upon herself to help me

book the musicians for the demo. "I'm getting you the best guys," she said. "So you can look to them for advice. If you get stuck, don't be ashamed to admit it. They'll guide you."

"Thanks, Ro," I replied. I picked up the enormous pile of lead sheets on her desk and headed for the copy room. "You're the best, you know that?"

"Abso-elvis-lutely, JJ," Rona replied. "All I ask is that you play it for Bobby ASAP so he'll get off my back about you delivering."

I scurried away. I had no intention of playing it for anyone until the right singer was about to record.

BY SIX THIRTY, I was exhausted. If I hadn't had Dulcie to look forward to, I would have gone home. I left my cubicle door open and noodled around with some arrangement ideas until she finally arrived.

"Brought you a little something to listen to, baby girl," she announced, setting a stack of 78 RPM records down on the piano. "This is just a small part of my collection. These are the ladies who taught me everything I know. I thought you might like to listen to them."

I stood up and flipped through the pile. I had read about these women, but I had never heard some of them sing. Dulcie's idols ranged from Bessie Smith to Alberta Hunter, from Blue Lu Barker to Billie Holiday, from Sister Rosetta Tharpe to Ruth Brown.

"I can't thank you enough," I gasped. "You know, I've always been fascinated by Rosetta Tharpe. I think it's 'cause I love her name. It's so poetic."

A shadow passed over Dulcie's face. "That's what I

named my little girl . . . Rosetta." Her voice caught. "I felt the same way. Rosetta is a beautiful name."

"Does your Rosetta live with you?" I asked, wondering what was wrong.

"My Rosetta's all grown up now, older than you. She's a grown woman. She lives here in New York, but it hasn't been right between us for a long time. We don't talk, but I know where she works, and maybe someday . . ." Her voice trailed off.

Her eyes clouded, and I took her hand.

"I'm so sorry I brought it up," I said.

"No worries," Dulcie assured me. She sniffed and straightened. "It is what it is, and it will be what it will be. Now let's get into my rehearsal. It ain't gonna take long."

"Why is that?"

"'Cause here's what I do. I sing the song down three times. After that it's in my bones, and it just gets stale. Got it?"

"I got it," I said, and that's what we did. I played, and Dulcie sang "I'm Glad I Did" three times. Each time better than the last.

"You happy with the way I sang it?" she asked.

"It's kind of perfect," I told her. "Now what?"

"Bobby got a record player in his office?"

"Sure he does."

Dulcie's face lit up. "Then let's go in there and play some music." She tucked the record stack under one arm and threw the other around my shoulders. We made ourselves comfortable in Bobby's office. He'd claimed he had the best speakers in the whole building, and maybe he did, because when I listened to Bessie Smith singing "St. Louis Blues," Billie Holiday telling the story of "Strange Fruit" and Ruth Brown wringing every painful emotion out of "I'll Get Along Somehow," I felt as if my ears had a direct connection to each singer's vocal chords.

Dulcie watched me, enjoying my delight. But after a few minutes, she whispered, "Gotta go and work. Take 'em home with you."

"I'll be very careful with them," I promised. "Let me meet you at your first office tomorrow night so I can help you get done in time for the demo."

"I start up at Hill and Range at six thirty," she said. "See you there."

I made sure not to leave a trace in Bobby's office to hint that anyone had been there.

FriDAY aT 6:20 P.M., I walked the stairs up to the top floor of the Brill Building, the home of Hill and Range Publishing. I wanted to avoid Nick and any end-of-the-week elevators down to the first floor, and I also wanted to help Dulcie finish her job. We were due to record "I'm Glad I Did" at nine, and I wanted her to feel relaxed, not hurried. And on the feeling-relaxed front, I decided not to tell her that Bernie Rubin was my uncle, or that the lyricist was the son of her ex-manager. I didn't want to distract her with memories of the past. If she asked who wrote the lyrics, I'd just tell her a boy I met in the building.

Luckily she didn't want to talk much at first. She wanted to hum. She said she did it to open her throat.

"You sure you want to help me?" Dulcie asked when she was warmed up.

I nodded eagerly, grabbing a mop from her.

"All right, then." Dulcie pulled out a cute little red Marvel transistor radio and tuned into "Murray the K's Swingin' Soiree" on WINS. The number-one song, "Sukiyaki," was in Japanese. Dulcie made up crazy lyrics to it, and we laughed our heads off. We harmonized to "It's My Party" by Leslie Gore and danced to "Da Doo Ron Ron" by The Crystals as we dusted and mopped. By 8:45 we had sung, danced and cleaned our way through all of the offices from Hill and Range to Good Music.

Even though Dulcie had to be about Janny's age, she somehow found a way to be forty-something and sixteen at the same time. She was the kind of person who made everything fun, even cleaning out a stranger's office.

"I wonder what my perfect brother would say if he could see me now," I said, almost to myself as I dropped the mop in the bucket. "He's known me all my life, but he doesn't know me at all."

"I know what it's like to have an older brother who's good at everything," Dulcie mused, her voice faraway. "Back home in Rocky Mount, my brother Lincoln was a football star. Now he's a university professor. He was born with the brains . . ." She turned away.

I opened my mouth, then closed it. It seemed to be another complicated relationship in her life. I was beginning to wonder why Dulcie didn't do well in the family relationship department. Then I thought about my own track record. If I was being honest, it wasn't so hot either. When I got up the nerve to ask her if she was married, she laughed that contagious laugh of hers.

"I almost had a go at it. But you are far too young for the language I would have to use to describe that mess. Plus I don't want to turn you off of marriage. Maybe it works for some people, but I figured out I'm not one of them."

"What do you mean?"

Her eyes twinkled. "I don't like people telling me what to do, and husbands have a way of doing that. Besides, the one I should have married, the one I wanted to . . . well, that's a whole other story for another time. Now you tell me about you. What are your folks like?"

I shrugged. "They're smart. Like your brother, I guess. But they don't understand me at all."

Dulcie shook her head. "I don't know about that. I do know that sometimes even though people don't understand you, they love you. They just love you in their own way."

CHAPTER FOURTEEN

B y the time we walked into Dick Charles Studios, I was
so high on my own happiness I couldn't top smiling.
Before now I'd only entered these hallowed halls to
deliver food and forgotten lead sheets. Tonight I was here
to actually produce a demo.

The first time I'd brought lunch to the writers, everyone
was in the control room, huddled over the recording console with the engineer. I was such a dunce that I thought if
I talked in the control room, it would get recorded. It took
a few trips before I realized you had to be in the recording
studio—the big room that you could see through the glass
window—in order for that to happen. Plus, a microphone
had to be turned on.

The studio was divided by sound baffles, cloth walls on
wheels that separated the drums from the bassist from the
guitarist. My smile widened when I saw that the musicians
Rona had hired were already there. Al Gorgoni was tuning
his guitar. He was an in-demand player even though he

was only in his early twenties, a gentle guy, already slightly balding, known for coming up with hooky guitar figures that complemented hits in the making. Buddy Salzman was the drummer. He played on most of The Four Seasons records, but still liked doing demos, even though they didn't pay as well. He just loved drumming and was as steady as a metronome. Then we had Russ Savakus on stand-up bass: a tall hipster with a porkpie hat who could lock in the groove and smoke a cigarette at the same time.

We recorded the music first, before the vocal, so I could let the guys go when I was done. That way I wouldn't go over my fifty-dollar demo budget. I introduced myself as I handed each one a chord sheet.

I was scared, but I had no time for fear. I matched their all-business attitude and headed for the piano. Once I started playing and singing, I felt a whole lot better. When I was less than halfway through, they began joining in. Even on the first run, they stayed with me when I slowed down and sped up. I knew I should have expected it, but experiencing it was different: it was as if they could feel what I was feeling. That's why they were "the guys."

Dulcie, meanwhile, settled in behind the board in the control room next to the engineer, Brooks Arthur. Like Bobby Goodman, Brooks was only twenty-four—and still, I knew, he was the engineer that everyone wanted. He was known for his great ears and mellow attitude. In less than half an hour, we had a take that both he and I were satisfied with.

Then Dulcie went out and stood behind the vocal mic, a Neumann U47, everyone's favorite. She casually put on her headphones, so she could hear the music track while she was singing.

"Oh, my," she murmured to herself, not realizing the mic was turned on. She fiddled with the gold note around her neck. "It's been too long."

I pushed the TALK BACK button on the console. "Let me hear you a capella," I told her. It seemed surreal that I was actually telling Dulcie Brown what to do in a recording studio. But then, everything about this night seemed surreal. She gave me a thumbs up and sang a few lines.

Brooks adjusted the levels and added just enough echo so she'd sound warm and intimate—but with enough edge so she could be inside the music track and still cut through. As Dulcie sang, he looked at me approvingly. "Nice pipes," he said.

"That's Sweet Dulcie Brown," I told him proudly. "She doesn't ordinarily do demos, but she's a friend of mine."

"You've got good taste in friends," Brooks said as he lowered the lights in the studio. "Let's give her some atmosphere."

Then he turned a knob and brought in the music we had just recorded. Dulcie began to sing along. He recorded her on a separate track so we could mix her in with the band later. He'd use another machine and bounce the music and vocal together to a third track so it would all sound seamless.

Her first take was good, but the next one was better. Take three blew us away completely. She owned the song by then. We didn't have to patch in a single line. By now I even felt at home with Brooks in the control room. I pressed the TALK BACK button and called her into the booth to be part of the decision-making process.

It was unanimous that the vocal couldn't get any better than take three. Even Dulcie was smiling at how great she sounded—and she was her own harshest critic.

It struck me then and there that there was no way any other singer was going to deliver what Dulcie gave us on that vocal. She was the one. Nobody else could give a performance as soulful, touching, and funky at the same time. The riffs and quirky turns were pure Dulcie; they were what made the song something more than the sum of its parts. She pulled every nuance out of the music and the lyrics. She made "I'm Glad I Did" sound better than I ever dreamed it could.

Suddenly I had an idea. Why couldn't this be Dulcie's comeback record? We could add strings or horns or whatever a record company might want later after they agreed to sign her. They could use what Brooks had captured tonight or we could record it all again if they wanted us to. It was pure gold. Sure, it was a young market, but Nat King Cole just had a Top-Ten record, and he was about Dulcie's age, maybe even older. It might be easier to sell someone young, but this song demanded someone who had lived and loved and suffered.

When Brooks ducked out for a cigarette break, I grabbed Dulcie's hands. "Let's use this to get you a new record deal," I whispered.

"You are somethin' else, baby girl," she said softly, squeezing back. "I love this song. But I want you to know that if you just use this as the demo to get another singer, I would still be grateful that I had the chance to sing it. Like the song says, I'm glad I did. You just go ahead and do what's best for you and your co-writer."

I threw my arms around her and hugged her. "Okay. But let's try to sell it with you. And if that doesn't work, we'll talk about it."

"Whatever you say, honey." Dulcie's lips quivered. I could see that she was holding in her excitement. Being in a recording studio again had awakened something in her; she had come alive. When Brooks got back, he ran a quick mix for Dulcie to take home. She tucked the acetate into her purse and turned to go.

Then she turned back. "Hey, JJ, girl, would you like to come to dinner at my place tomorrow night and listen to more of my record collection?"

"Are you kidding? I'd love to. What can I bring?"

"Just bring your sweet self. And your appetite." Dulcie jotted down her address for me. "Seven o'clock."

"I'll be there."

After she left, Brooks and I played with the mix until we ran out of time. Then he cut a record for me to take home.

Tonight was the best night of my life, I said to myself as I left the studio. I was sure tomorrow night would be even better. I didn't know then what a blessing it was not to know what the future has in store for us.

CHAPTER FIFTEEN

The next morning I played the demo as soon as I woke up. I got dressed moving and humming to it. I'd barely slept, but I felt wide awake.

Music can do that to you. There was a knock on the door. Janny opened without waiting for a response, as was her style. I raced over and turned down the volume. "I've hardly seen you all week and you just missed breakfast," she pointed out.

Uh-oh. For the first time since I'd started my job, I'd violated the Green Family Rule Number One. Not even Jeffrey did that unless he gave advance warning or was ill.

"Did you work until all hours last night?" she pressed.

"I sort of did," I confessed.

She folded her arms across her chest. "Tell me how it's going."

"Really well. I recorded my first demo last night. Would you like to hear it?"

She glanced over her shoulder. Today was Saturday. Of course—it was her shopping day. I could almost hear the siren of a Bergdorf Goodman sale calling out to her. "Of course I would," she said, looking at her watch. "How long is it?"

"Two minutes and forty seconds."

"Let's do it, then."

I raced back to the record player and dropped the needle on the first groove. As "I'm Glad I Did" filled the room, I watched her face. To her credit, she really listened. Her brow was knit in concentration. On the other hand, I could tell that she didn't get it at all. There wasn't a flicker of emotion in her entire being.

"That's lovely, dear," she said when it was over. I could almost hear the silent sigh of relief. "A very nice song."

"Nice?" I would have preferred she hated it. At least hatred involves passion.

She looked me in the eye. "JJ, know you have talent, and you can write very catchy melodies. I hope that by the end of the summer, you'll see that you can use the brains you've been given for something more."

"Mom, we have our deal," I responded, matching her glare. "Let's not discuss it anymore. I just wanted you to hear what I was doing."

"And I did," she said. "Now I'm off. Your dad and I are going to see *Enter Laughing* tonight. I'm meeting him for dinner before the show, and we're joining Susan and Marshall for drinks afterward, so we'll be home late. Since we didn't see you at breakfast, can you tell me your plans?"

I ignored her curt tone and brightened mine. "Someone in my office is having a listening party, and I was invited." It wasn't a total lie.

"Have fun." And with that Janny was gone.

I LISTENED TO THE demo about ten more times once I had the apartment to myself. Then I fooled around on the piano, began another melody I kind of liked, and watched the afternoon melt into evening.

At six o'clock, I put on some lipstick and headed for the subway. I boarded at 59th Street. By the time the train passed 96th Street, I realized that I was the only white person in the car. There were a few Negro girls my age seated across from me. One of them shot me a look of such hostility that I couldn't help but swallow as I looked down at my feet. It hadn't dawned on me that I might not be welcome in Dulcie's world. There was no barrier between us. Music was our connection. But as I rode to 125th and Lexington, I realized that it wasn't that simple. The world outside the Brill Building, outside of music, hadn't caught up to Dulcie and me. I was an outsider on this train.

Fortunately, Dulcie's apartment building was just a few blocks from the station. I glanced at the piece of paper she'd given me—152 E. 126th Street, apartment 606—and picked up my pace. I kept my head down. I couldn't wait to talk to her about some ideas I had for the arrangement of her actual record. I was sure we'd be back in a studio in no time once a record company heard what she could do. My plan was to play the demo for Bobby on Monday.

I knew from experience that he was bright-eyed, bushy-tailed and ready to rock and roll when the week began. True, I still had to run my plans for Dulcie's comeback by my co-writer. But once Luke heard the demo, he would have no choice but to agree.

I smiled to myself as I turned the corner onto Dulcie's block. Luke knew how pushy I could be . . . in a good way.

I paused.

The street was cordoned off and surrounded by police cars. Their flashing lights threw streaks of red and white across a sea of anxious faces. People were milling around, asking what was going on. I frowned, trying to peer around the crowd. Getting through this mess was going to make me late for dinner.

I stood there for a minute, not knowing what to do. Something on the sidewalk was covered by a yellow tarp.

Then to my surprise, I caught sight of a familiar face: Frank McGrath. He was an NYPD detective Mom had known since she'd worked as a law clerk right after her graduation from law school. He'd been a beat cop back then, but they had stayed friends over the years, and his family had occasionally come to dinner at our place. He was a few pounds heavier, and his hair was a bit thinner than when I'd last seen him last, but he had the same craggy, weather-beaten face.

"Frank!" I called to him. "It's JJ Green."

His eyes narrowed as they peered toward me. McGrath was as shocked to see me as I was to see him. He made his way over to me. "What are you doing here, JJ?"

"I have a friend who lives in the building. I came to have dinner with her."

"I'll walk you in." He lifted the yellow tape so I could slide under.

"What's going on?" I asked.

"Some colored woman jumped from the sixth floor," he said.

I stopped. "My friend is colored, and she lives on the sixth floor." I said. The words filled me with dread. The night was hot and humid, but still I shivered. I had a terrible feeling in my gut.

"Hey, so do fifteen other women," he replied, ushering me along. "This building is half colored, half Hispanic. Just go on up and enjoy your dinner."

I shook my head, my eyes flashing back to the yellow tarp. "Please, Frank, can I see?" My voice sounded hollow in my ears, as if someone else had asked the question. "Let me see the woman who jumped."

"JJ, you don't want to do that," he said firmly.

I turned to him and grabbed his arm. "Please," I said. "Please, just let me see her face. I have to see her face."

He bit the inside of his cheek, but he could see the desperation in my eyes. "This is against the rules. Don't ever tell your mother I did this," he muttered.

His face was grim as we approached the tarp. I felt dizzy and looked up to see a young woman nearby weeping. Her face looked strangely familiar. Crouching beside the tarp, McGrath pulled it back just enough to reveal the face of the jumper.

The world went black.

This is what it feels like to die, I thought.

My knees got weak. I couldn't breathe. I felt everything slipping away.

It was Dulcie.

The blood had pooled under her head, and her eyes were closed. I heard someone moan and realized it was me. The sidewalk came rushing up at me, and Frank caught me before I hit the concrete. In a dizzy haze, I felt myself being walked to a police cruiser and eased down into the backseat. I kept thinking I was going to wake up but I didn't. I was awake, and this was real. It couldn't be, but it was.

Dulcie Brown was dead.

I sat there, feeling nothing, feeling dead myself. Someone placed a paper cup of water in my hand.

"Drink this, JJ," McGrath said. "Do you want me to have one of my guys take you home?"

"No, thanks," I choked out. "I'll be okay."

I gulped some water. I tried to get the image of Dulcie lying on the pavement out of my head. There was something about my glimpse of her that struck me as strange, maybe even wrong, but I couldn't bear to think about it. I pushed it out of my mind. I had to go home.

"Please don't mention this to my folks," I whispered to McGrath, forcing myself to get out of the car.

"I won't," he promised. "You sure you're all right?"

I nodded and shambled away, still carrying the cup of water. An elderly Puerto Rican woman stood apart from the crowd, sobbing. She looked up as I ducked under the tape, and we connected for an instant.

"¿La conocía?" I asked. *Did you know her?*

"She was my neighbor and my friend. I heard her screaming as she fell. I'll never forget that sound." She spoke in Spanish, barely a whisper.

I put my arm around her and held the cup to her lips so she could take a sip. "*Señora*," I whispered, "she was my friend, too. Did you see or hear anything before she fell?"

"She was yelling at someone," the woman said. "I can't remember what she was saying. I didn't pay attention. I thought it was none of my business, so I just turned up the TV."

I pointed to McGrath. "If you remember anything, tell him," I told her.

"I don't like police," she whispered. "I'm not legal."

"I understand," I answered. "Then call me if you remember anything. Okay?" I scribbled my name and the Good Music phone number on the paper cup and handed it to her. "Will you do that?"

She nodded. "Was she a good friend to you?" she asked.

"She was more than that." I almost choked on the words. "She was a mother to me, my music mother."

CHaPTer SIXTeeN

The next morning, I experienced that weird moment when you wake up after something terrible has happened, and for an instant life is normal. It's just another morning. But then your pain hits you as hard as it did the first time, maybe even harder. I knew I needed to stay out of my family's way, because I couldn't guarantee that I wouldn't fall apart. So I broke Green Rule Number One for the second morning in a row and left a note saying I was having breakfast with my friend Rona from the office, and that we were going shopping and to a movie.

Then I went and hid in a movie theater by myself.

Cleopatra was playing. It ran about four hours. I sat through it two and a half times, but I couldn't tell you what it was about, because the movie in my head was playing *The Too-Short History of Dulcie and JJ*, over and over. I kept reliving every moment we shared. Was I responsible in some way for her death? Would she still be alive if I hadn't talked her into recording our song? Maybe by bringing her back to the studio, I'd also brought back the horrible memories of her drug addiction, failure, and loss. Maybe she couldn't handle all of that again. The final straw could have been that "I'm Glad I Did" would be part of a comeback strategy.

Was she so fragile that the idea of being a recording artist again pushed her out that window?

But the more I thought about it, the more I began to wonder why Frank McGrath was so quick to write off Dulcie's death as a suicide. She knew I was coming over to dinner. Why would she choose that time to jump? She was genuinely happy when she'd left the studio, the kind of happy that a person can't fake. Besides, the Hispanic lady had heard an argument before Dulcie had jumped. And something had seemed wrong about her when I saw her lying there . . .

Then it hit me. *The necklace.*

Her neck was bare. The gold note necklace was missing. I had never seen her without it until then. It wasn't valuable enough to kill for. But why she would take it off before she jumped?

When I finally got home, I headed straight for my room and dove into bed. When Janny asked if I was all right, I told her I thought I was coming down with something, and I just needed to sleep. Maybe she didn't believe me, or maybe she was just too fed up to bother pressing me. She left me alone, and that was all that mattered.

I MADE IT THROUGH breakfast on Monday by not talking and pretending I was under the weather—maybe I'd eaten something bad with my friend Rona—but would try to tough it out through work.

It wasn't until lunch with Bernie that I finally lost it. Marla had decided to join us on this day, and I was glad she was there. I wasn't sure how Bernie would react, if he'd even give a damn. I knew, though, that whatever happened, Marla would know how to handle it. And I could share the tragedy with someone who knew Dulcie. Besides, Bernie had a right to know. He'd given Dulcie her start.

As soon as our plates were in front of us, I began to tell them that I had become friends with someone he used to manage. But the moment I said her name, I dissolved in tears. I managed to choke out, "Dulcie Brown is dead."

Bernie and Marla exchanged a glance across the table. "What are you talking about?" he demanded.

And then everything tumbled out: how I'd overheard her sing, how she'd heard me play, how we'd come together in a magical moment to record a demo—and the next night she'd thrown herself from her own apartment window. My voice was hoarse.

Bernie's face crumbled. He downed his vodka stinger in one gulp and held up his empty glass for the waiter to bring him another. "I can't believe it," he whispered. "She was a tortured soul, but she was strong." His voice was thick. "And she was a good woman."

Marla's eyes grew misty. It was clear to me that she couldn't bear seeing Bernie in pain. She covered his hand with her own. "It's not your fault, sweetie," she whispered. She turned to me. "Bernie always felt guilty about deserting Dulcie when she was out of control. But what else could he do? She wasn't able to work. She was embarrassing herself and him, and she wouldn't listen to anyone." She turned back to Bernie. "Please, honey, don't beat yourself up."

I shook my head. "But she got past all that. She was working as a cleaning lady in the building. That's how I met her. Did you know that, Uncle Bernie?"

Bernie swallowed hard. He took a slug of his fresh drink. "Justice, baby, did she know I was your uncle?"

"I didn't have a chance to tell her. I was going to tell her that night . . ."

"Bernie," Marla whispered, "people do what they have to do. Dulcie did what she had to do, and so did you."

Bernie downed the next drink just as quickly and held up his glass for a refill. I decided to excuse myself. I didn't want to watch my uncle drink himself into oblivion. And I knew Marla could handle him better without an audience. I promised to get in touch soon. Besides, I wanted to play the demo for Luke. He deserved to hear it. He deserved to hear the miracle Dulcie had performed with his lyrics as soon as he could.

Of course, my face gave me away as soon as I stepped in Nick's "office." He looked at me intently as he closed the elevator door. "Everything okay, kiddo?" he asked gently.

I spilled everything once more. To my surprise, when I described how Detective McGrath had pulled the tarp away to reveal Dulcie's face, Nick's eyes welled up. "I knew Dulcie," he murmured.

"You did?"

"Yeah, she asked me some questions when she first began working in the building. I knew her big hit record. I was a real fan of hers. And I knew she was trying to clean up her act. In fact, sometimes when I worked double shifts, I'd drive her home. It was on the way to the Bronx. She used to ask me to come up so she could give me some money for the gas I used getting her home. Can you believe that? I said no, though, 'cause I'm a gentleman. I was afraid people in her building might talk, you know?"

I choked back my tears. Dulcie had no idea how many people adored and respected her.

Nick turned the crank. "Anyway, I'm sorry, kiddo. Where to? Eight?"

I shook my head, patting the demo in my purse. "Seven, please."

I COULDN'T DECIDE WHETHER to tell Luke what had happened before or after I played the demo for him. I half hoped he wouldn't be there so I could drop it through the mail slot and not have to deal with explanations.

I knocked softly. If he didn't answer I'd leave it and scoot. I never thought I'd be less than happy to hear his voice. But my heart dropped when he answered, "Come in."

He didn't sound as if he were in the greatest place either.

I opened the door tentatively.

Luke was sitting on a packed carton hunched over what appeared to be a stack of legal papers. His white shirt was grubby and rolled up at the sleeves.

"Hey," he said, making an effort to look welcoming and not succeeding. He stood and his brow furrowed. "JJ, are you all right?"

"Not really," I admitted. I pulled the demo out of my bag. "Listen to this first. I'll explain everything when the song is over."

He took the record, slipped it carefully out of its sleeve and retreated to the record player at the back of the room.

"Actually before you play it, I want to say something—"

"It's okay if you screwed it up," he interrupted over his shoulder. "We'll just do it again together."

"It's not about the demo," I told him. "Before you play it, I just wanted to thank you for the words. I thought I was okay at lyrics until Bobby told me I wasn't. Then when I read yours, I knew what he meant. I grew up loving folk music and musical theater, so that's where my lyrics tend to go. They're either too 'Kumbaya' or too 'Bad Larry Hart.' So I want you to know how grateful I am to you for sharing those words with me."

Luke turned to face me. I think he actually blushed a bit. "I'm sure you're better than you or Bobby thinks you are. I just wrote what I felt. I know that if you did that, if you wrote from your heart, you'd be fine."

"You may have a more Top-Forty-type heart," I cracked.

"I'll take that as a compliment," he answered dryly. "Can I play this now?"

"You can. I'm dying to know what you think of it."

He clicked on the power and dropped the needle on the vinyl. For the next two minutes and forty seconds, we stood there listening. I could tell by the look on his face that he was listening not only with his ears but with his entire being, his soul.

When the last note faded, he asked if he could play it

again. This time, I could see a more detached look on his face, though he couldn't keep his head from swaying in time. He was a music mogul's son, after all; I could tell that now he was sussing out the demo as a sales tool, now that he knew how amazing it truly was.

"Why that face, JJ?" he asked once the song was over. "You did a great job."

I shook my head. If I opened my mouth, I knew I'd start crying again.

"I hated not being there, but the truth is I didn't need to be," he went on. "There's nothing I would have done differently. Dulcie's performance . . . there are no words for it. Everything fits: the song, the track, the singer—it's perfect. It's one of the best demos I've ever heard. And believe me, I know. My dad used to bring home plenty of them. So what's wrong?"

"I don't know how to tell you this, so I'll just say it," I blurted out. "The night after the demo, I went to have dinner with Dulcie at her place. When I got there, she was lying dead on the street. They say she threw herself out her own window . . ."

"My God," he whispered, sitting down on a packed carton.

For a moment, we were both quiet.

"I'm so sorry, JJ," he whispered. "That must have been terrible for you. I don't understand. Was she back on drugs?"

"I don't believe she was," I answered, collapsing onto a carton across from him. "She wasn't high on anything but music when we worked on the demo. I had all these fantasies that I could get her a record deal from this performance, and she might be able to make a comeback. She was excited about it and happy."

Luke chewed a nail. "I can't even imagine what you must be going through right now. Is that the whole story?"

I nodded. "It doesn't make sense, does it?"

"No, it doesn't," he said firmly. He looked at me. "You say she was happy the night before. Happy people tend to keep on living if they can. Did she say anything that could have hinted at something bad in her life?"

"I don't know," I said. I sniffed and wiped my eyes. "I've been too upset to think about this clearly. There was this woman, a neighbor, who said she heard Dulcie fighting with someone before she jumped. But the woman won't go to the police because she's an illegal. And Dulcie said some things that made it sound like she had some secrets. I figured it was just stuff from her past. You know how drugs can mess up family relationships. She had a daughter things weren't right with. A brother . . . I don't know."

We both sat there staring into space, thinking. Then Luke's eyes flashed to a stack of ledgers on his desk. "I have to ask you something," he said. "What do you know about your Uncle Bernie? Are you two close?"

I shrugged. "Not until now. I've only really gotten to know him this summer. I know he's got a rotten reputation, but he's been really good to me. My mom hates him. They're so different sometimes I can't even believe they're related."

Again, he almost smiled. "It's funny you said related. Remember how you said, we're kind of related?"

"Yeah, but the key words are 'kind of,'" I said quickly. "I only said it 'cause your dad and my uncle were partners. It was a bad joke, really, that's all it was. It's not like we're actually related." *I'm the bad joke*, I thought. *I'm babbling like an idiot.*

"I know, I know," Luke soothed. "I meant that we have a connection through our families, the music business, and now through this song. I guess what I mean is . . . I hardly know you, but you took my lyrics and turned them into something I never could have imagined. You saw something in those words I didn't see myself. And now . . ." He stood and began pacing around the messy office. "JJ, there's something I have to share with someone, and you're the only person it makes sense to share it with."

I swallowed nervously. My mind was darting all over the place. He was going to tell me that he felt something for me. I knew I couldn't be the only one in this equation.

"What is it?" I asked. My voice trembled.

"I've been going through royalty statements and payment schedules that go back a long time, all the way to the forties."

I blinked. Confessions about feelings don't begin with a sentence like that.

"And from the way I read them," Luke continued, "my dad and your uncle had a habit of not paying their artists their rightful share. It looks to me like they put their names as writers on songs they had no part in writing. And there were two sets of books."

My mouth was suddenly dry. "What are you saying?"

"That they ripped off a whole lot of people, including Dulcie Brown."

"Are you sure?" I whispered.

"I'm not an accountant, but a lot of what I've found is self-explanatory," Luke said, his voice strained. "I'm going to have someone check everything out, but I have to tell you, from what I see, all their writers and recording artists have a lot of money coming to them." He looked down. "I feel lousy for everyone, including me. If this is true, a lot of the money my dad left me really belongs to other people. I can't live with that."

For the first time I noticed the dark circles that ringed those bright eyes. His chinos were rumpled. He looked as if he'd slept in his clothes—if he'd slept at all.

"My dad was all I had," he went on. "I never knew my mother. She died right after I was born. I looked up to him. He was my idol, and now I see that he may have made a mess of his own life and the lives of everyone around him."

I couldn't stop myself. I reached out and took his hand. "I'm so sorry," I said. "I know what it feels like to care about someone who isn't who you'd like them to be. It may not stop you from loving them, but it sure has a way of screwing up your head."

I let his hand go even though I didn't want to.

He looked at me. His eyes had softened to jade. "You get it," he said. He smiled a little half-hearted smile.

My heart soared for an instant. "I do," I told him. I checked my watch. My lunch break had ended, but the rest of our conversation was unfinished. "Luke, why would someone invite a friend for dinner if she was planning to kill herself?"

"The answer is, she wouldn't," he said softly.

"I've been thinking the same thing," I told him, and with that I was out the door.

CHAPTER SEVENTEEN

The next morning dawned with breakfast as usual at the Green apartment. Everyone was seated in their usual seats. They were going through their usual breakfast routine, and it struck me that their world hadn't changed at all, while mine had been shaken to its core. My parents had no idea of my pain and loss, and there was no possible way to tell them.

Janny had finished the main section of *The New York Times*. She was treating herself to the Fashion and Style section in an appropriate outfit: an Oleg Cassini double-breasted pale lemon A-line dress. Jeff's nose was embedded in the local news. He wore his usual short-sleeved shirt and boring tie. My father, dapper in a summer seersucker suit, was flipping through the main section Janny had passed to him. They all looked so perfect, so comfortable.

Jules peered over a headline that read PRESIDENT HAILED BY OVER A MILLION IN VISIT TO BERLIN. "I'm just reading back here on page forty-four about some singer who killed herself in Harlem," he mused. "You'll be thrilled to know, Janny, that Bernie was mentioned in the article."

I swallowed my orange juice with a gulp. "What does it say about him?"

"Just that he used to manage her." His tone was matter-of-fact. "Justice, have you ever heard of someone called Sweet Dulcie Brown?"

Before I could stop myself, I jumped up and ran around to see the paper.

Jeff chimed in as usual. "You must have heard of her, Irving. You know every singer who ever sang a note."

I skimmed the article over my father's shoulder. There was a publicity picture of Dulcie at the height of her fame. She was wearing a sequined dress and a choker with a red rose at her throat. She was so slender and young, glancing back over one bare shoulder seductively. She had the magic; you could see it in her eyes.

"I vaguely remember her," Janny remarked. "One more example of what the music business does to people. Another poor druggie gone. So sad. Pass the jam, please."

I wanted to scream, "That's not who she was!" But what good would it do? What difference would it make to Janny, who had already slipped Dulcie into her category of low-life people who didn't matter?

"Yeah, I knew who she was," I said to my brother, my voice flat. And I did. And if I was honest with myself, the woman I knew would not have killed herself. She was upbeat, she was drug free, and she never took off her necklace. Unless . . .

That wasn't who she was. Maybe like Luke's father or

Uncle Bernie, there was another side to her. A darker side. No matter what I felt in my heart, I hadn't really known her for that long.

Maybe everything I believed was wrong.

Janny stood up. "JJ, do you want a lift to work?" she asked. "I'm going your way."

"No, thanks," I told her. "I'll take the bus."

I BURIED MYSELF IN work at Good Music, digging into my usual routine of copying, filing, checking demo costs and delivering coffee. When Rona asked about the demo session she'd set up for me, I managed to hold it together. I told her the truth: it went really well. I promised to play the song for her when we both had time—which I was sure wouldn't be soon, since we were both always overloaded. Her job was protecting and scheduling Bobby, and mine was mindless grunt work.

Even though I had graduated to compiling a master list of studios, musicians and demo singers, my mind had plenty of free time to go crazy with speculation about Dulcie's death. I had to be careful not to let my tears stain my composite list. I was engrossed in organizing the list and wiping my eyes when Rona stuck her head in the door.

"You have a call, JJ," she said.

I glanced at the clock, puzzled. It was eleven thirty. "Who is it?"

"He didn't tell me his name. You can take it at my desk, but make it short."

I followed her to the big room and picked up the phone at her desk. "Hello, this is JJ."

"Hi, it's Luke. I have something to tell you." His voice was hurried and scratchy, even more tired-sounding than usual.

My heart skipped a few beats. "What's going on?"

"This morning I got a call from Dulcie's landlord. He was cleaning out her apartment and found a box under a loose floorboard in the closet. It turned out to be an auto-biography Dulcie was writing."

I gasped. Rona looked up at me. I managed a weak smile.

"Listen to the dedication, JJ," Luke went on. "'To George Silver, the music man who gave me my break, my career and my greatest happiness.'" He paused for a second for me to take that in. "The landlord looked up our office number and called me."

"Are you going over to get it?" I asked, struggling to process.

"I already did. It's here in my hands. I thought you might want to come down and read it with me. Can you make it for lunch?"

My throat tightened. I wasn't sure why I felt like crying, other than Luke's decency seemed unreal. *He actually was waiting for me.*

Rona had taken her seat at the desk and was staring me down for tying up her line.

"I really can't. I have to work through lunch to get stuff done, but if you want to go ahead—"

"I won't read it without you," he interrupted. "I know what she meant to you. Can you come down after work?"

I swallowed. "You'd wait that long for me?"

"Of course I would. But get here as fast as you can."

"I will," I promised. I put the phone back on its cradle and headed back to my office.

"Everything okay?" Rona called after me.

"Absolutely," I lied.

"It's going to be one of those days, isn't it?" she added.

You don't know the half of it, I thought, closing the door behind me.

CHAPTER EIGHTEEN

At 6:01, Luke and I were sitting side by side on the couch in George Silver's office, surrounded by boxes filed with the possible evidence of a lifetime of deceit. Stacked on a carton in front of us was the memoir: *Living the Blues* by Dulcina Brown.

For a moment, we just stared at the cover page.

"You go first and pass the pages to me," I suggested.

Luke nodded. It was a good thing he was a fast reader. I wondered if he was as frightened as I was of what we might find out.

My mama was only a baby herself when she had her first baby. My brother Lincoln was born three years before me, when Mama was only thirteen years old. By the time I came along on February 9, 1920, Lincoln's father was long gone. I had a different daddy than Lincoln, but he didn't bother to stick around either.

So you could say that my bad history with members of the opposite sex began before I was even born.

Since Mama had two kids and no one to turn to, her mama, Annie Mae, took us all to live with her. Now, you might say, isn't that wonderful, isn't that kind, what a loving woman to offer a home to a young girl and her babies. Well, I can tell you that my grandma Annie Mae Brown was none of those things. She didn't have a wonderful, loving, or kind bone in her body. She was judgmental, bossy, and mean.

Her husband, Dustin "Dusty" Brown, was a clarinet player. He spent most of his life on the road so he wouldn't have to live at home with Annie Mae.

We all figured out why pretty quick.

Grandpa Dusty had been taken in by her good looks, of course. She had skin the color of coffee with plenty of cream, huge hazel eyes, and lots of curves even though she was skinny. But he learned like we did that nobody looks good when they're beating you in the head with a broom, her favorite thing to do when he came home late. So he figured it was best not to come home at all.

He sent her a few dollars now and then, even though Annie Mae didn't need his money. She earned her living working as a maid for a white family in town. I think she bossed them around, too, but she was such a good cleaner that they never complained. Or maybe they were just afraid of her like the rest of us.

When I was seven, Mama ran away with a traveling Bible salesman. You can imagine how desperately she wanted to escape for her to do that. Now, Bible salesmen may be fast talkers, but all their talk is about salvation. Maybe she thought she'd find it with him. You can imagine her mama's reaction when Mama went missing. I think they must have heard my grandma cursing all the way to Raleigh, sixty miles away. From then on it was just my brother and me, playing Survive Annie Mae.

If I hadn't had Lincoln to take care of me, I don't know what I would have done. Lincoln was just about the best big brother any girl could ask for. He'd take me with him to football practice so I wouldn't have to go to Mrs. Royster's when Annie Mae was at work.

Mrs. Royster took care of everyone's kids at her house after school. But someone was always getting hurt or getting into a fight. So my brother took me with him and sat me on the sidelines, where I played with my dolls and watched him become a great quarterback.

Luke glanced at me. I wondered if he was thinking what I was thinking. I decided to ask. "I kind of want to get to the music stuff, don't you?"

"You read my mind," he answered.

We skimmed the chapters that followed. In them Dulcie recounted her life as a kid in a small North Carolina town and her relationship with Lincoln, the brother she worshipped, the only male role model in her life. He more than lived up to that responsibility. He nurtured and respected her. While other big brothers either cussed out or had no use for their baby sisters, Lincoln treated little Dulcie with both affection and respect. It was a mystery where he got his smarts and his manners, but he was the boy in town that everyone wanted their son to be like and their daughter to be with. Lincoln was the star of the high school football team, and Dulcie was at every game cheering for him. There wasn't a boy in school who could come close to Lincoln in looks, grades, character, and athletic ability.

"Well," I said to Luke as he flipped ahead. "Grandma was a pisser, and both parents taking off was not a good beginning. Good thing she had the brother, huh?"

"He sounds a little *too* perfect," Luke responded evenly.

"Here comes a good part."

The next chapter was titled "Finding My Voice."

Grandma took us to church every Sunday. It wasn't so much about religion for her. Annie Mae played the piano for the choir, and she liked to show off, so she was always decked out in her finest. She had real musical talent. She would sit us down in the first row and proudly take her seat behind a broken-down upright, hammering away at the keys, even the ones that didn't work. She told us that if she had one wish it would be for a real organ to play in church. I believed her. It never would have occurred to her to wish for a better life for us. Annie Mae was all about Annie Mae.

Bessie Wallace, who was sixteen, was given all the solos. She had the best voice in town and she knew it.

Then one day she came down with a bad cold. She swore to the choir director that she was well enough to sing each and every solo in "Oh Happy Day." But when she opened her mouth for the first verse, nothing came out. Not knowing what to do, Bessie burst into tears, ran down the aisle and out of the church. By the time the next solo part came around and the hubbub had died down, people began to look toward Bessie's sister, Edna, who was about my age.

When Edna stepped up front, I don't know what came over me. I jumped up onstage and before she could open her mouth, I began to sing. I was only ten, but I knew somehow I could do it. I just let the words and music come through me and added some curly turns that I liked. Sure enough, the faces of the congregation told me I was not only doing it, I was killing it. By the end of "Oh Happy Day," I was the new star of the Ebenezer Baptist Church Choir. After that Bessie had to share all the solos with me even though I was just a skinny little kid.

Sharing the stage taught Bessie about humility. I felt bad for her, but it taught me that if you think you can do something, you probably can. That day after church, Lincoln carried me all the way home on his shoulders like I had made a touchdown or something.

"Why didn't you tell me you could sing?" Grandma Annie Mae asked me when we were alone.

"You never asked me," I answered.

She hit me upside the head. "Don't you sass me, missy."

I wasn't being sassy. I was just telling her the truth. She knew nothing about me except that I hated green beans, but I figured I'd best shut up. I never told her anything about who I really was. She never knew that I sang whenever I was alone, or that I made up songs in my own head. She never would have cared, besides.

There was a knock at the door. I looked at Luke, puzzled.

"I ordered Chinese food from Ruby Foo's," he said. "I figured we'd be here through dinner."

I began digging through my handbag. "I'm paying for half of this one."

He stood and stretched. "You know, most girls like having their dinner paid for."

"I'm not most girls," I shot back, pressing two dollars into his hand.

He rolled his eyes but took the money to pay the delivery man. As we spread out the cartons on boxes we'd pushed together, Luke paused for a second. "I like that about you, you know."

"Like what?"

"That you're not like most girls."

I flushed, not knowing what to say. Best just to eat. I hadn't realized how hungry I was until we began digging our chopsticks into the steaming white boxes, trying not to get sweet-and-sour sauce on Dulcie's life story. Luke flipped ahead looking for mention of his father. But he stopped on a chapter called "Losing Lincoln."

He glanced at me. I nodded. It was only a single page.

My brother Lincoln was a man I could believe in. Until his senior year in high school, he could do no wrong. Linc was getting ready for his finals. He had accepted a full athletic scholarship to play for the Buckeyes at Ohio State. It was an accomplishment almost unheard of in those days for a colored boy. I had never been as proud of anyone in my life. I knew I had a lot to live up to being Lincoln Brown's baby sister, but I was ready.

Thanks to him, I had something to prove. I would never have had the courage to take over "Oh Happy Day" if I didn't have my brother as an example. He never let anything stand in his way. I wanted to be a star just like him. Then I found out something that destroyed my faith in him.

It's easy to do the right thing when you have nothing to lose. I watched my brother and waited to see what would happen when he was tested. He failed.

I had nowhere to turn. He had always been my refuge, but now I had no refuge. I watched him graduate with honors. I don't know if he knew what I knew. I made up my mind not to reveal anything to anyone, even to him. And I haven't to this day. Maybe he wondered why we drifted apart. I couldn't look at him in the same way from then on. Still, I've kept his secret. When the right time comes, he will have to be the one to tell the world who he is. Every person must account for his or her own truth, including Lincoln.

"What the hell could that be about?" I asked. "What did she find out?"

Luke put down the page and shoved his carton of food aside. "The worst is yet to come," he muttered. "She hasn't even met George and Bernie yet."

"I know." I bit my lip. "Do you want to stop for a while? I'm a little afraid to go on reading."

He shook his head. "I'm more afraid not to."

I nodded. We closed the unfinished containers of Chinese food as the skies darkened outside. The next chapter was called "Getting Out."

After Lincoln left for college, Marcus Waters became the new quarterback at school. He was handsome and a great athlete, but any resemblance to Lincoln ended there. Marcus was a bad boy, the boy you would least like your daughter to be with. He did everything he wasn't supposed to do. He smoked, he drank, he fooled around with something called dust. In whatever spare time he had, he broke every heart in sight.

Annie Mae warned me that he was trouble and she would take a strap to me if I ever took up with him. But he was so fine, I couldn't help myself. Every girl in school wanted to be with him, and he wanted me. Before Annie Mae could even figure out what was happening, Marcus and me were doing everything together, and I mean everything.

That winter I found out I was pregnant. The summer before my sophomore year I had a baby girl. I was fifteen, a year younger than my mama was when she had me. To carry on the family tradition of desertion, Marcus and his family moved away. Annie Mae swore she'd track him to wherever he moved to and beat him to death with her broom. When I told her not to bother, that I never expected him to stick around, she considered taking the broom to me. But she reconsidered when she realized that if I wasn't around, she'd have to take care of the baby herself.

I named my little girl Rosetta after a singer I saw at a revival meeting. She played guitar and sang in a way that made people cry. She bared her soul with every note. She might have been the bravest woman I ever laid eyes on.

It was then I realized what I had to do. That woman made me understand that if I was going to do right by my

*baby, if I was going to get out of the lifeless life I was living,
my voice was the only weapon I had to fight my way out of
nowhere.*

"She was right about that," Luke said, glancing up.
"What else could she count on?"

"Nothing," I murmured.

After that the pace of the writing picked up. It was as if
Dulcie wanted to race through that part of her life because
it was so painful. It was full of misspellings and sentences
that ran on and on, but it sang with the passion that con-
sumed her, the passion to break away from the legacy of
failure passed down by the women in her family.

Dulcie had to quit school to take care of Rosetta because
Annie Mae insisted that she pay room and board as if she
were a tenant, not family. The new mother and her grandmother were at each other's throats most of the time.
Dulcie sang at clubs in Raleigh and Charlotte and as far
away as Nashville and Knoxville. She graduated from bad
boys to bad men. She was hurt and discarded, undervalued
and underpaid, used and misused, but she kept on working
with any band she could at night, improving her voice and
repertoire. It was the only way she could pay Annie Mae and
still be home every day to take care of Rosetta.

She kept on this way until Rosetta turned six and was
old enough to go to school. Dulcie hated doing what she
had to do next, but she rationalized that there was no
other way if they were to stand a chance. If they were ever
to get out of the rut they were in. Besides, abandonment
had been seared into her soul. Part of her believed it was

her destiny to commit the same crime. So she took off for New York City, leaving Rosetta with Annie Mae.

It was 1942, the war was on, and I was singing at Minton's Playhouse on 118th Street in Harlem. A cat I knew from home named Thelonius Monk was the keyboard player, and he got me the gig with the house band. They even learned a few of my songs and let me sing them. I was barely getting by, missing Rosetta and feeling ready to throw in the towel, when one night a cool blond dude with crazy green eyes asked me to join him at his table.

That man was George Silver.

George brought me over to meet his partner, Bernie Rubin. They were starting a music publishing and management company, and they were interested in signing me. They told me that they liked my songs and my sound and thought they could get me a record deal. Nobody else was busting down my door, so I said okay.

The next day I signed a whole bunch of papers they gave me. Then I played them every song I'd written. The two of them kept smiling at each other. Then they took me out and bought me some really nice dresses and shoes. Once I was all dolled up, they brought me over to sing at a record company. George was especially nice to me. I liked him better than Bernie, who was a little bit gruff. Within a couple of weeks they had a session booked for me for a song I hadn't written called "Swing Time."

I didn't like it too much, but George said the record company told them that I had to record it. The bosses there told George and Bernie that colored girls like Ella never sang their own songs, so I shouldn't either. What they didn't tell me was that the record company owned the publishing rights to the song they loved so much. That's why they loved it. They were going to collect all the money if it was a hit.

It wasn't a hit, and Bernie got all crazy, ranting and raving that my songs were better. George had to calm him down. George was the only person in the world that Bernie would ever listen to. I think he could have calmed down a pack of werewolves if he just talked to them. He was the most charming man I'd ever met.

Before you know it, he had charmed me. I really liked him. In fact, I more than liked him. He had a tiny limp, because when he was a kid he'd broken his leg, and it was set wrong. That made him 4F, and it also made him seem even more special. He was a very tender man.

I felt pretty bad about the record being a bomb. George was the only one who knew why I was so sad, why I couldn't bounce back. He knew what the record meant to me. It wasn't about becoming a star. It was about being able to bring my little girl to live with me.

One night he came to the club alone and walked me home with his arm around my shoulder. People stared to see a white man walking like that with a colored girl, and some of them said mean things, but he didn't care. He came upstairs and we talked. After that, I guess you could say we made beautiful music together. That was how my falling in love with him began.

I turned to Luke. The sun had long since set. Dulcie's pages and Luke's troubled face were only illuminated by the green shaded desk lamp across the room.

"Wow," I said. "George and Dulcie. Did you know about that?"

"No, I didn't." Luke's eyes and voice were distant. "That must have been before he met my mother."

"Was your mom a singer?" I asked.

"Yeah, a background singer. Her name was Gina La Russo. She died right after I was born. Dad never talked about her very much. Just said she was a good woman and very talented. He thought I looked like her, but I never saw it."

"Did you ever see a picture of her?"

Luke pulled a black-and-white snapshot out of his wallet. To tell you the truth, it looked almost like a prop, like the kind of photo a manufacturer puts in a wallet to show people how neatly photos fit in. Luke's mom had dark curly hair. To me, she looked like a pretty Spanish or Italian girl—but aside from the hair, I agreed with him; they didn't look alike at all.

"She's pretty," I said.

"I guess," Luke answered. He shoved his wallet back into his pocket and picked up the stack of papers where we'd left off.

Bernie knew about George and me. It was hard to keep it a secret. He could tell by the way I looked at George. He told us both to just keep it quiet. We were something no one wanted to talk about.

Once when I went to drop a demo off at George's apartment building on Central Park West, they told me to go up in the service car. They just assumed that I was the maid.

Instead of making a fuss, that's what I did. I knew we had no future. But I couldn't stop seeing him because he was my manager, and I couldn't stop loving him because he was George.

My career was going nowhere until I played George and Bernie a song I wrote called "Good Love Gone Bad." They both got excited. I was so glad because I was excited, too. Something about it felt special and right for me. They said they were sure it was a hit.

Things didn't go smoothly, though. It almost didn't get made. George and Bernie had to fight with the record company and convince them to let me record it. I was the writer of the words and music, and George and Bernie's company published it, and both of them produced the record. That meant they hired the arranger and told everyone in the studio what to do. When it was all done, they had me sing a song the record company president wrote to put on the B side, and somehow with that they managed to satisfy everyone.

And everything just got better. George and Bernie were right. The record of "Good Love Gone Bad" was a smash hit.

It went all the way to number one on every chart in Billboard *and* Cashbox.

First time I heard my voice on the radio singing my own song, I almost cried from happiness. The first time I saw my name on a marquee, I jumped up and down like a little girl.

And the first time someone recognized me on the street and asked for my autograph, I almost fainted.

George told me I should treat myself to something nice.

He knew I didn't understand banking and money, but he made sure I had everything I needed whenever I needed it. First thing I did was send the Ebenezer Baptist Church a brand-new organ, and I made sure Annie Mae knew it was from me. I had a little gold plaque made and attached it to the side where the congregation could see it. It said, This organ is a gift from Dulcina Brown, granddaughter of Annie Mae Brown, organist of the Ebenezer Baptist Church.

Then my life in New York got crazy because the record company and my managers wanted me to go on the road and work and make money. I wanted to stay home and write and be with George. The road was hell. Everything down south was segregated. The trains had colored only and whites only cars. I traveled with a piano player, and he hired musicians in the different towns we played in. I got to come back to New York only when the record company decided they wanted me to record again.

I didn't care, though. I was just happy to be back with George. I kept promising myself that I'd bring Rosetta up to live with me as soon as my life got settled.

Then I started feeling sick. I was tired all the time. It was summertime, and New York was hot as hell, and I figured that's why.

But it wasn't. I was pregnant.

We kept it hidden for as long as we could. Then George pulled me off the road. He and Bernie made up this story about how I'd gotten into a car accident and needed time to recover. I had a feeling Bernie hated me after that. He hated me for not getting an abortion. He knew these doctors who would do it. But George wanted our child as badly as I did, even though we knew we'd never be able to raise it together.

All of a sudden, Luke drew in a sharp breath. He doubled over as if in pain. "Oh, my God," he said in a terrible whisper. "Oh, my God." He dropped the page he was reading and buried his face in his hands.

"Luke? What is it?" My heart started pounding. I picked up the page, but before I could read it, he lifted his head and looked at me, his eyes watering. His olive skin had turned sallow.

"My dad lied. He lied . . ." The words stuck in his throat, but he forced himself to speak. "He never told me who I really was. Not even when he knew he was going to die. Don't you see, JJ? It's written right there. Dulcie Brown was my mother."

CHAPTER NINETEEN

What do you do when you find out you aren't who you thought you were? When you find out that the person you trusted most in the world lied to you? When your life collapses around you?

And how do you help someone when all these things happen at once?

I had no answers for any of these questions, and no one to ask, as I looked into Luke's ravaged eyes. Everything he had taken for granted had been ripped away from him, gone the instant he read the words that came next on that page.

Our baby boy, Luke, was born December 10, 1944, at Lenox Hill Hospital.

I didn't know what to do, so I did what came naturally. I put my arms around him and held him close. We sat that way for a very long time. Neither of us said a word. There were no words to say.

My mind spun with thoughts of Dulcie. All the *what ifs*. What if I had decided to tell her the name of the lyricist?

That the words she loved, the song she had sung had been written by Luke Silver, her son? What would she have done? Would she have admitted the truth to Luke, or would she have continued to hide the fact of who he was and who she was to him? Could she have found out somehow? Could it have been a factor in her taking her own life? But no, only he and I knew.

I glanced at my watch. It was almost eight thirty. Eleven o'clock suddenly seemed very close.

Finally Luke pulled away from me. "I have to keep reading," he said, his voice hoarse. "You don't have to stay."

"I want to stay," I told him. "We can't stop now."

Our baby boy, Luke, was born on December 10, 1944, at Lenox Hill Hospital. I knew there was no way we could raise him together. In the south, there were still separate waiting rooms and ticket windows in bus stations for Negroes and whites, and it was even illegal for them to just live together. In New York City, segregation wasn't that out in the open, but the races were not supposed to mix. It wasn't even until two years later that Jackie Robinson would be hired to play for the Brooklyn Dodgers baseball team.

George and I had created a person together out of our love, but we had made a child who had no real place in the world. So we came up with a plan. It tore my heart out, but it was the only thing we could do. Although my name was on the birth certificate as the mother, George promised me he'd get one with another name on it. We agreed that I would be able to visit Luke but would never tell him who I was. I would just be a friend of his father.

If his skin remained light enough, he would never know that his mother was a Negro. If his skin turned dark, George would tell him he was adopted. I prayed he would look like George and never know the pain of being a colored person.

We were lucky that George had enough money and connections to take care of everything that needed to be taken care of. He found a false "mother" and got the birth certificate altered. The woman was a white backup singer he had known for years who was dying from a brain tumor. It was tragic and wrong of us, but she never even knew. She passed away four weeks to the day after Luke was born.

Maybe I was wrong, too, in keeping my son's heritage a secret. I was not ashamed of who he was, and neither was George, but the world was not ready for him. It still may not be, even as I write this in the year 1962, but I pray every night that soon that day will come. I hope I live long enough to see it so I can take Luke in my arms and tell him how much his mother loves him and has always loved him.

Luke sat there without making a sound. I held out my hand and he took it. There was no one in the world but the two of us. Even if eleven o'clock came and went, I knew I wouldn't abandon him if he weren't ready to be left alone, no matter what the price I paid at home.

"I don't remember her ever coming to see me," he murmured. "I wonder if she did."

"I don't think we remember much of anything before we're three. Actually, my mother told me that when she was arguing some case where it was brought into evidence." I sighed. "Dulcie might have come before then."

"Maybe she'll tell us." He picked up the remaining stack of pages.

I ached for my children, the one I'd left behind and the one I could never hold, and I hated my life. I hated having to hide my relationship with the man I loved. I couldn't come up with anything that sounded like a hit song, so I felt I was letting George down. The record company was driving him and Bernie nuts, pressuring them for another hit. Bernie knew about Luke, of course, so he understood why I couldn't concentrate. But he wasn't exactly sympathetic. Bernie was all business and told me I had to write a follow-up to "Good Love Gone Bad" and record it, or the record buying public would forget me.

"Get off your beautiful ass and get the job done," he used to say.

I wanted to do what he said. I wanted it more than I'd even wanted that first hit. When I finally wrote another song that everyone liked, I didn't know whether we'd waited too long to release it. Or maybe it just wasn't as good as we thought it was. It barely crawled onto the charts and hung there by its fingertips. Each record after that did a little worse, and I began feeling a lot worse about myself.

One night after a session, one of the musicians saw how low I was and offered me some of that dust that Marcus used to use. This cat called it nose candy. "Take a snort," he said. "You'll feel better, and you won't get hooked." So I

thought, Why not? *I needed relief from this feeling inside, this ache that wouldn't fade.*
I did feel better for a little while, he was right about that.
But that's all he was right about.

I glanced at Luke, unsure of how he would feel about reading about the intimate details of his mother's slide into drug addiction. He picked up the pace, skimming a little, but he never stopped handing the pages to me.

Dulcie went on about how she began to depend on cocaine to pick her up when she was down and how she would crash after the cocaine wore off, so the cycle would begin again. She always needed more to pick her up. She hit up George for cash. She threw fits when he refused to feed her habit by not giving her money. She knew she was behaving badly, not showing up for shows or record sessions on time or in such bad shape that her voice sounded "like sandpaper," but she couldn't help herself. She couldn't stop.

When the record company dropped her, Bernie flipped out. He said George could handle her alone. Bernie was done with Dulcie Brown, and even George forbade her to see Luke while she was using. He thought that might get her to quit. But not being able to see her son just made her feel so terrible that she used even more. Finally, George was unable to get her a deal, unable to book her, and ultimately unable to deal with the junkie she had become. In the end, he gave up like Bernie and refused to manage her—although he continued to give her money to keep her from starving or becoming homeless.

It was now 1951. Sweet Dulcie Brown thought she'd lost everything she had to lose.

I don't remember much of the next few years, but in 1952 or early '53, I was singing at a dive up in Harlem. To tell you the truth, I was not doing that much singing. What I was doing a lot of was sitting with customers, pushing cheap champagne and occasionally going home with one of them. I was a mess. When I had cocaine, I was on a manic high, and when I didn't have it, I was so far down the gutter looked like up to me.

That was the year my sixteen-year-old baby girl, Rosetta, decided to run away from home and come to visit me. Her timing couldn't have been worse. She came to find the mother she dreamed about all her life, someone who would open loving arms and hold her close. She deserved a mother like that. But I couldn't take care of myself, much less take care of her.

For as long as I live, I'll have to live with the look in her eyes when I gave her a bus ticket back to North Carolina and dropped her off at the Greyhound Station. I don't know if she took that bus, but I know that I lost her back then. I wish I could go back and talk to that girl. To tell her that today, after four years of being clean, I am ready to be the mother she wanted. Maybe I still can make things right. I only hope I'm not too late.

Luke rubbed his eyes. He looked drained.

"Those are the words of someone with a plan for the future," I said. Then I bit my lip, wondering if I'd said the wrong thing. Luke had every reason to be enraged at both his father and his mother. He had every reason to toss her manuscript and her memory into the garbage, along with his father's paper trail of fraud and deception. "You're right." Luke said, his voice weary. "I don't believe Dulcie killed herself, and if she didn't, I want to find out what really happened to her."

I stared at him a moment. "You're really brave," I whispered.

"You think?" he asked with a sad half-smile. "Because right now I feel scared to death."

"Listen, Luke," I told him, "I'm with you on this. I need to know what happened to her, too. I hadn't known her that long, but there was something . . . I loved her. That's as plain as I can put it. I loved the Dulcie I knew."

Luke looked into my eyes. It seemed as if he had aged a few years in just a few hours. He took my hand. "We haven't known each other very long either," he said softly. "But I don't know what I would have done without you tonight."

All I could do was nod in agreement. The truth was, I was scared to death, too. Not only of what I'd find out about Dulcie, but of what I felt for Luke Silver.

"Then we're in this together?" Luke whispered in the silence.

"You don't know how together," I breathed as I squeezed his hand back. Afraid of what I'd do if I lingered an instant longer, I let go and stood. "Now, I gotta get home by eleven, or I turn into a bagel."

In spite of everything, he smiled. Damn, that smile felt good.

I smiled back and raced out the door.

CHapTer TWeNTY

as clueless and unfeeling as my family might be, I don't think I ever appreciated them as much as I did that night. The smell of the apartment, cigarettes, the brandy, the sound of legal chatter was more comforting than I ever dreamed it could be. I poked my head into the living room to let them know I was home and wished everyone good night.

"Sleep well, sweetheart," my dad called after me.

If I only could have. I lay there staring at the dark ceiling, picturing Luke alone in his father's empty apartment. He had left there this morning a white boy and returned at night half Negro. How would that affect the rest of his life? Had he graduated from high school like me? Maybe . . . he was eighteen and a half. Which one? Was he going to college? Was it anywhere near Barnard?

The thought of not seeing him made my stomach tighten. What if the college found out about his background? Would he still be welcome?

He was still Luke to me. Still a boy I was drawn to no matter what his heritage. He was just Luke Silver. That's all he had to be for me to feel the way I felt about him. But would it change his feelings toward me? I knew that he felt something for me. But I didn't know what that something was. If it was just friendship that would be okay . . . not good but okay.

I shuddered, twisting, and throwing off the covers. I didn't care that his mother was colored. But others certainly would. Some would assume he'd always known and tried to "pass" for white. The difference was that I knew the truth, and so did he. What would that truth mean to him? Could he even figure that out yet?

No doubt he was tossing in his bed, unable to sleep, just as I was.

THE NEXT DAY AT Good Music, when I heard the different writing teams cheering, I knew Bobby had posted the chart positions. At least some of the songs had moved up with a "bullet." The bullet was a red dot next to the title, indicating it had one of the biggest gains in sales that week. The teams whose songs and fallen or stalled on the charts pretended they were happy for their pals—but none of them were going to win any Oscars for their "happy face" performances.

Tacked to the Good Music bulletin board, next to the charts from *Cashbox* and *Billboard*, was the updated list of singer-producer teams who needed new songs. When the crowd had cleared, I checked to see if there was anybody who could possibly sing what Luke and I had written.

Leslie Gore was looking for a follow-up to "It's My Party" with Quincy Jones producing. Ruby & the Romantics were looking for another "Our Day Will Come" with Al Stanton producing. Neither was right for "I'm Glad I Did." The rest of the singers needing material were male singers or groups. So this week was a big no.

Nobody fit our song, and our song didn't fit anybody.

But I wouldn't give up, especially not now. Part of me felt I owed it to Dulcie to see this song through—at least the Dulcie Brown who'd brought magic to our demo. Besides, this song was still my only chance at keeping my dream alive. I knew I had to be patient. And I'd learned from Bernie that part of getting lucky was timing. I could wait.

If I played our song for Bobby too soon, it would be old to him by the time the right singer came around. Bernie's lessons in song placement strategy had not been lost on me. Namely, if Bobby liked the song, it was important for him to believe that the casting of "I'm Glad I Did" was his idea. No matter who put the song and singer together, he would eventually remember it as being his idea if it was a hit. But if he thought it was his idea *before* it was a hit, he'd make every effort to be sure it became one.

At five forty-five, I was just thinking about what kind of food to bring so I could work through dinner when Rona stuck her head in.

"JJ," she announced in a dry voice, "your popularity is overwhelming. But getting calls here is not a good idea."

"I wish I had a little phone I could carry around with me, but nobody's invented it yet," I said, trying to make her laugh.

"Very funny," she croaked. Rona was always hoarse by the end of the day. Snapping at people on the phone all day took it its toll. "I would yell at you, but I have no voice left," she whispered as I picked up the phone at her desk. "Hello?"

"I found Rosetta Brown," Luke told me breathlessly.

I blinked. "Wow. Tell me the truth, you're really a detective. This writer-publisher thing is just a cover?"

He chuckled lightly. "Actually, I found out through Nick. Of course he knew Dulcie. He knows everyone who works in this building, so I asked if he knew anything about her daughter. Seems that Dulcie told him a few months ago that Rosetta was working as a waitress at Birdland. She never got up the guts to go and see her, Nick's words. So I called, and she's still there."

My gaze turned to Rona, who was glaring at me. "Uh . . . wow," I said.

"Turns out Thelonious Monk got Rosetta the job. Can you believe it? *The* Thelonius Monk. But we already knew he knew Dulcie from Rocky Mount—anyway, sometimes they let Rosetta sing. I think we should go there and talk to her."

"Okay," I said, but my voice was uncertain. I wasn't sure that popping in on the child Dulcie had abandoned was the best idea.

"Look, JJ, the book ended right when Dulcie got her job cleaning offices in the Brill Building a year ago. Doesn't it seem weird that she would end up in the building where her ex-managers worked? There's a year of her life we have to fill in. I want to talk to everyone we can find who can help us do that, so I'm going to Birdland tonight. You don't have to go with me—"

"Like hell I don't," I answered, before I could even formulate my thoughts. "If you're Sherlock, I wanna be Watson."

Rona wrote a message she held up for me to read. *If you're role-playing with a boyfriend, my phone is not the place to do it.*

"Meet you at seven in front of Birdland," Luke said, and I could almost hear his smile. "And Watson, don't be late."

THE EVENING HAD TURNED hot and sticky when I met Luke in front of the legendary club on 52nd Street, named for Charlie "Bird" Parker. Like so many others, he'd died too young, thanks to his addiction—but unlike most, his music was eternal. Entering the vast, dark, smoky room was like stepping into a time machine. It felt like the forties, the heyday of jazz.

Luke and I took a minute to breathe it all in. It wasn't very crowded; Birdland was more of a late-night spot. The empty stage glowed in a haze of cigarette smoke. The few men seated at the bar all looked like Bernie, slick and well dressed. Posters for jazz greats adorned the walls near the entrance: Dizzy Gillespie, John Coltrane, and Thelonious Monk himself.

The hostess, a beautiful dark-skinned woman in a black dress, approached us. "We don't serve minors," she told us.

"We just want soft drinks," Luke responded. "We'd like to talk to Rosetta Brown."

"You some kind of junior reporters?" she asked suspiciously.

Luke shook his head. "No, we knew her mother."

"You can sit there," the hostess said, indicating a nearby table. "That's one of her tables." Then she disappeared.

Luke avoided my eyes as we slid into our chairs. And then I realized something: Rosetta was his half-sister. This was far more complicated than anything I could ever imagine or understand. For once I promised myself I would try to keep quiet. I doubted it would work out. There was too much I needed to know.

I recognized Rosetta the moment she walked toward us. She had Dulcie's high cheekbones and skinny curves, but there was something more. She seemed familiar, as if I'd seen her before. But was that possible? Then as she moved closer, I gasped. Luke looked at me, and I pointed to my throat. Around Rosetta's neck was a gold note on a chain. Just like the one Dulcie always wore.

"I got a break coming right up," she told us by way of hello. Her voice and eyes were cold. "I know you're too young to be reporters. After I bring your order, I can talk for a few minutes, and that's all the time I got to give. So what do you want?"

"Um . . . two Cokes, please," Luke said. "And we won't take too much of your time."

As she walked away, we followed her with our eyes. "Where did she get that necklace?" I muttered.

"Why does it matter?" Luke asked.

"Because Dulcie had one just like it, and it was missing the night she died."

Luke's eyes widened a bit. We sat in silence for a minute
or two. He finally opened his mouth to say something, but
Rosetta had returned. She plunked our drinks down in
front of us, sat down, and lit a cigarette. "Listen," she said,
"I've had all kinds of people droppin' in to talk to me since
my mama's name was in the newspaper. None of them had
anything good on their minds. Mostly they'd figured out
all kinds of ways to use me and my mama's memory. So
just tell me flat out what you want, and I'll tell you why you
can't have it."

I took a sip of my soda, mostly out of nervousness.

"I understand why you're suspicious," Luke said sin-
cerely. "But honestly, we don't want anything except to
talk to you."

"I met your mother and worked with her on a song,"
I blurted out in spite of myself. "She sang the demo for
me, and I really cared about her. I'm not sure that she
killed herself. If she didn't, I want to find out what happened."

"Well, if you find out, give me a call," Rosetta said,
staring right back at me. Her voice had an edge. She
inhaled and blew out a cloud of smoke. "I spent a lot of
years hating that woman. She dumped me twice. As far as
I can tell, she was a crazy junkie, and the only person she
cared about was herself. Funny how life works out, though.
Some things run in the family." She smiled mirthlessly and
tapped her cigarette on the ashtray.

Luke and I exchanged a quick glance across the table.
"What do you mean?" he asked.

"I didn't know what to do to kill the hurt she left inside

of me, so I did what she did. I started takin' stuff to make me feel better. Trouble is, it only made me feel worse."

"Listen to me, Rosetta," Luke said, leaning toward her. "There's something you should read. Your mother wrote a book about her life. She wrote about you and her feelings for you. If you want to see the pages about you, I'll make a copy and drop them off for you. I know she hurt you, but she never meant to."

Rosetta peered at Luke through the fog of cigarette smoke that surrounded her. "How did *you* get my mama's book?"

I stiffened, holding my breath.

Without missing a beat, Luke replied, "My dad managed Dulcie with her uncle"—he jerked his head toward me—"and she dedicated it to my dad. When the landlord found it, after she died, he gave it to me."

"Smart man," Rosetta snapped sarcastically. "Didn't he know managers always steal from their clients? Especially when they're uneducated colored women. So this dude decides to give her book to the son of the guy who ripped her off and left her broke."

I concentrated on my soda again, stewing with questions. So Rosetta knew Dulcie had been ripped off. Was she just hipper than Dulcie? Or had Dulcie chosen to forgive George?

"I didn't know about any of that until now," Luke answered. He held Rosetta's gaze. "Believe me, I'm embarrassed and shocked by what he did. I'm going to find a way to repay the artists who were cheated."

Rosetta snickered. "Yeah, I know. The check is in

the mail. Look here, you two. I've been clean for seven months. I'm tryin' not to hate on my mother. Tryin' to forgive her for what she did. It's part of the twelve steps to recovery." She took a final drag and stubbed out her cigarette. "I wanted to see her, but I never got to. That's all I got to say."

The hostess came over and tapped Rosetta on the shoulder. She looked up and nodded. "You know where you can find me," she said as she got up. "If you find out anything new, let me know. I'd be curious to find out what happened."

She vanished through a door near the side of the stage.

"What do you think?" I asked Luke. "Do you believe she's clean?"

"I don't know," he mused. He took a sip of his drink and leaned back in his chair. "There's always that old question: How do you know an addict is lying? The answer: their lips are moving."

I nodded, then shook my head. "I can't figure out why she looks so familiar. It's not just that she looks like Dulcie. Where have I seen her before?"

Luke shrugged. His eyes wandered back to the closed stage door.

"Listen, I need to ask you something," I said. "Why didn't you tell her you two are related?"

His jaw flickered. "I'm not ready yet," he whispered.

"I get it. I shouldn't have asked."

"No, it's okay," he said. But his voice was hollow.

For a few minutes, we sat in silence and finished our drinks. He didn't seem in a hurry to leave, and I didn't want to push him. I was just reaching in my purse for money to settle the bill when the house lights dimmed. A silky baritone boomed from the speaker system. "And now Mr. Thelonious Monk would like you to meet a special young lady with a great voice, Miss Rosetta Brown."

Luke shot a glance at me. The sparse crowd offered some quiet applause. I stared as Rosetta stepped up to the mic, glowing in a spotlight. Before I could fully grasp what was happening, she'd begun to sing "Good Love Gone Bad."

It was clear from the first few notes that she was her mother's daughter. She had Dulcie's throaty voice—that same quirky blues phrasing, the same ability to turn a song into something more, into a dramatic experience. Like Dulcie, she sang from her soul. By the end of the song, tears were rolling down her cheeks.

The applause was much louder now. She tried to smile and nod. That's when it hit me. It was like a flashback. That face . . . the tears.

"Luke," I whispered, clutching his arm, "now I know where I saw her before. It was in the crowd, on the street, that night Dulcie died. Rosetta was there. And she was crying then, too."

CHAPTER TWENTY-ONE

The next morning, Jules had a 7:30 A.M. "meeting in chambers." If one of his cases could be resolved before trial, it provided one of the very few legitimate reasons for him to violate Green Rule Number One. I wished I could have gotten my mother alone without my "I can never mind my own business" brother, but this was as good as it was going to get, and the timing was crucial. The moment Janny put down her newspaper and Juana left to refill her coffee cup, I asked the question that had been burning inside me since last night.

"Mom, do you consider yourself someone who knows a lot about suicide and murder?"

"And good morning to you, too, dear," she answered dryly.

"Wow, Irving," my brother the jerk declared, "which one are you considering?"

"Probably murder if you keep sticking your nose into everything," I grumbled.

"Please, kids," Janny breathed, throwing Jeff a look. "The answer to your question, JJ, is that being a criminal attorney, I know more than the average person. But you know that already. Why do you ask?"

I shoved my muffin aside. "I'm interested in knowing how often the police make an assumption that a death is suicide when, in fact, it might be murder."

Janny's face brightened. "So glad to see you taking an interest in criminal matters, Justice. In my opinion, the police often go into 'suicide mode' and make careless assumptions if a case appears open and shut." She smiled as Juana placed a fresh cup of coffee in front of her, and she took a sip. "It depends on the victim, of course. Sometimes the police get caught when the medical examiner's findings prove that it's a homicide. But very occasionally, if there is no autopsy, someone can literally get away with murder."

"If I'm found dead," Jeff chimed in, "the first person to suspect is my sister."

"Shouldn't all deaths be considered homicide until the facts rule it out?" I asked, ignoring him.

"Of course they should," Janny said. "But that isn't always the way it works with an understaffed police department in a big city. It often depends on the victim. For instance, if a vagrant is found dead, there's not going to be an intense search for his killer. On the other hand, a dead politician might cause a lot of hoopla and a big investigation."

I nodded, processing her words in terms of what it might mean for Dulcie. "Who'd be in charge of the investigation?"

"Every death should be investigated by a police detective, but it doesn't always happen that way. Sometimes patrol officers on the scene are allowed to take charge when suicide seems clear and the department is overloaded."

"But shouldn't the victim's state of mind make a difference in determining if it was suicide?"

Janny's smile widened, but her brow was knit. "Of course it should. JJ, you're impressing me." She was clearly loving this conversation. She hadn't been this interested in what I had to say since I uttered my first word at ten months. "Now tell me, where is all this coming from? Really?"

I took a deep breath and leaned back. Even Jeff had decided to stop needling me. He looked just as bewildered as Janny.

"It's about the suicide of Dulcie Brown, the singer. I knew her. She cleaned the building where I work. And she didn't strike me as someone who would kill herself."

Janny sighed. "Look, JJ, I'm sorry this woman passed away, but I must say, I am not surprised. A drug addict singer who ends up a cleaning lady is exactly the type of person I knew you would run into in the music business. And that was another reason why—"

"I know, Mom," I cut in. "But she wasn't on drugs anymore. She hadn't been for years."

"She might have had a relapse," Jeff suggested brightly.

"Thank you, Jeffrey," I snarled, without bothering to look at him. "Your input is always appreciated."

"You're really upset about this, aren't you?" Janny asked. Her tone softened ever so slightly.

"I am," I admitted. "I didn't even want to tell you I knew her."

My mom thought a moment as she took a final sip of coffee. "The article said she jumped out of a window, right? In my experience, women rarely kill themselves that way. Too violent, too frightening. They usually choose pills or carbon monoxide, but someone on drugs . . ." She shrugged. "She might have fallen out the window in a stupor."

I shook my head. "I've been looking into it, and I read somewhere that one of the neighbors heard her screaming as she fell. That's been haunting me."

"Screaming," Janny remarked. "That's strange. I've been told jumpers almost never scream. You remember Frank McGrath, don't you? He was the one who mentioned that to me."

My heart nearly jumped out of my chest. *Frank McGrath?*

"Mom," I managed, "thank you. This has been one of the most enlightening conversations we've ever had." And with that I folded my napkin, kissed my mother on the cheek, patted Jeff on the head just to annoy him and steeled myself for another long day at the Brill Building.

CHAPTER TWENTY-TWO

I knew Luke would be expecting me after work. I couldn't wait to tell him about my conversation with Janny. I didn't bother with the elevator; it would be too crowded. Instead, I took the stairs and exploded into Luke's office—only to find someone sitting on the couch, one of the few surfaces not covered with paper or cartons.

It was Nick. Damn. Still, I put on a big smile.

"Hi, JJ," Luke greeted me from his perch on the edge of the desk. I could tell by his fake-casual voice that something was up. "Nick's taking a dinner break and telling me stories about my dad and your uncle."

I got it. Luke was on a mission to find information about his father and Dulcie any way he could. I knew that this was the time to summon my rarely used patience. If I hadn't been able to keep my mouth shut last night, I could redeem myself now. Nick grinned at me, flashing strands of corned beef stuck between his teeth. He slugged down the rest of his Dr. Brown's cream soda.

"Hey, kiddo, did your uncle ever tell you about him and George and Gamblers Anonymous? You know GA?"

"Um . . . no," I answered. I couldn't have cared less, but I figured he'd be gone faster if he had the chance to tell his story.

"Well, they'd both lost so much money on the horses that they had to sell a few of their record companies. That's when they decided they needed to join GA. They told me they thought they might have a gambling problem. They 'thought'"—Nick made air quotes—"that's funny right there. Anyways, they found a GA meeting in an office building a few blocks from here. The two of them set off with the best of intentions. I know they did, because in the elevator they practiced saying, 'My name is Bernie, and my name is George, and I am a gambler.' Only trouble was, once they got to the building and got on the other elevator, they thought it would be a great idea to bet on what floors it would stop on. Everyone in the elevator made a bet. Turns out they were all GA members. They went up and down, winning and losing until the GA meeting broke."

Nick burst out laughing. Luke shot a glance at me.

"So instead of getting help, George and Bernie got every other degenerate gambler to start gambling again," Nick added. "They felt bad. They swore they'd go back the following week and try again. I don't think they did, though. The two of them were something else."

Luke laughed, but I could tell it wasn't real. This was another part of his father's secret life. "No, I don't think my dad ever did go back to GA," he said after a moment.

"I remember guys who looked like Nathan Detroit from *Guys and Dolls* showing up at our place regularly and my dad handing over envelopes."

"Bernie and George were characters, all right," Nick declared. "They were what made this building exciting." He got up and headed for the door. "So long, kiddos," he called back. "See you in my office."

I waited until I heard the door close. "What was that about?" I whispered.

"He knows a lot about my dad." Luke replied simply. "The more stories he tells the more I find out."

"That's what I figured." I took Nick's spot on the couch. "So listen, I had a talk with my family's resident criminal expert about suicide. My mom says, first of all, women rarely jump out windows to kill themselves. They're much more likely to take pills. It's less violent and scary. And two, jumpers never scream. That woman at the scene told me she heard Dulcie screaming all the way down. I was thinking of taking these thoughts of mine to Frank McGrath. He's this cop my mom knows who happened to be the detective at the scene. What do you say?"

"I'm a step ahead of you, Watson," Luke said. "Chow down, because we have a meeting at eight tonight with Dulcie's brother, Lincoln Brown."

My mouth fell open. "What? How?"

"It was easy, actually," Luke said with a shrug. "And don't get me wrong. I think going to the police is a good idea. But I'm not sure the police will pay any attention to us unless we have some concrete evidence to show them. The more we can tell them, the more believable we become.

So I did a little research and I tracked down Dulcie's not-so-perfect brother. He had a pretty great football career at Ohio State, and there weren't many Negro college players back then. Tracking him down was no problem. Guess where he is."

"Columbus? Cleveland? Oh, just tell me."

"He's here in New York City. He's one of two colored academics teaching at NYU."

I leaned back in the couch. "How'd you convince him to meet? Did you tell him who you were? You know, that you're related?"

"Hardly. My dear Watson, you and I are writing an article for our high school newspaper about Negroes in academia. We want to encourage our colored classmates to pursue higher education and academic careers."

I almost laughed. "And he bought that?"

"Sleuthing is only one of my many talents." Luke flashed a sly grin. "Acting is another."

I wanted to hug him, but I controlled my impulse. "May I suggest we take the subway, Sherlock? I turn into a pumpkin at eleven."

"I thought you turned into a bagel," Luke said.

"Haven't you ever heard of a pumpkin bagel?"

"Remind me never to eat at your house, Watson," he said. And there was that smile.

AS FAR AS MY family was concerned, NYU was considered a failsafe school, not in the same league as Barnard. I hadn't even bothered to apply. But when I got down there, I had to admit that I was pretty impressed. For one thing, the campus was in the Village, right near some great clubs, and the faculty buildings were nicer than those I'd seen at Barnard. Professor Brown's office was at the top of a steep carpeted stairwell on the second floor of an elegant brownstone near Washington Square Park.

We were ushered into his office by an adoring female student intern not much older than we were. Dulcie's brother was standing behind his desk when she introduced us, and it was obvious by the look in her eyes that she worshipped him. I had a feeling all his students, both male and female, looked up to him in the same way. He *was* an imposing figure, cool and elegant in a tweed jacket and bowtie. At forty-six, he had retained his athletic build and was well over six feet tall. The family resemblance was clear the second we laid eyes on him: he shared Dulcie's razor-sharp cheekbones and hazel eyes.

"Thanks for agreeing to meet with us on such short notice, Professor Brown," Luke said, extending a hand. "I'm Luke Silver. This is the classmate I mentioned over the phone, JJ Green."

I shook Professor Brown's hand. He graciously asked us to sit down, indicating two wooden chairs facing his desk. "I must say I'm a bit surprised, Luke," he said, leaning back. "I was expecting to see Negro students writing this article."

There was a breath of silence. "I'm half Negro, Mr. Brown."

The professor's eyes briefly shifted to me. "I see." He smiled warmly. "Now what would you like to know about me that you believe will inspire your classmates?"

"We've researched your academic career," Luke answered. "And we promise we won't take too much of your time. We know you're a busy man. But we would be interested in knowing more about your early life and family relationships. Young people like us are interested in knowing how that affected the direction you took. For instance, we know that your sister, Dulcie Brown, was once a successful singer and songwriter. Can you tell us a little bit about your relationship with her?"

Professor Brown winced. "Are you aware that she just passed away?" he asked in a low voice.

Luke nodded. "I read about it in the paper. My condolences. It was one of the reasons I contacted you. I am sorry for your loss."

"Thank you," Professor Brown said gruffly. For a moment I wondered if he was going to ask us to leave. But Luke plowed forward.

"We couldn't help but wonder about the different paths your lives had taken. We'd like to know how to encourage our peers to look to you as a role model."

Professor Brown clasped his hands together. His eyes wandered to his bookshelves. "We grew up in a small town in North Carolina, and I loved my little sister very much. I took her under my wing. I tried to be a father to her as well as a brother. She needed that. I suppose we both did. But once I left home for college, I couldn't stay connected to her as much as I wanted to, and eventually we drifted apart."

Luke nodded at me. That was my cue. I reached into my handbag and pulled out a notebook and pencil, per what we'd rehearsed. We wanted to look legitimate, and taking notes would do that. It would also help us remember what he said.

"I know that she had a troubled life," Luke continued. "It contrasts so strongly with yours. You went from college football star to a brilliant career in academia. Why do you think you navigated your life so smoothly and she had so many struggles?"

Professor Brown sighed and closed his eyes as if searching for an answer in his memories. His forehead was tightly creased.

"I don't know," he said softly. "Perhaps it helped that I'm a man. It's easier for men, even colored men. I can only tell you that when she was lost in drug abuse, I tried to help. She rejected my efforts. She held on to a disagreement we had years ago and wouldn't forgive or forget. It broke my heart to see her in a hell of her own making." His eyes opened. "When she finally killed herself, I almost felt relief that she was out of her pain."

"Did you know that she was writing a memoir?" Luke asked.

Professor Brown hesitated and for an instant I wondered if Luke had pushed his luck too far. "Yes, she called me wanting to know some information about our mother's family history. I told her what I knew."

I saw by his face that something else had gone on in that conversation. Something that was still hurtful. I made a note of it.

"Professor Brown, what else can you tell us about your youth that you believe might be helpful to our readers?" I asked to keep the interview charade going.

Relieved, he launched into a history of his high school and college years, presenting himself as "someone who was always focused on the future, and what he could do in the present to attain his goals." He stressed community work, integrity, and a proper balance of work and play. He put forth the usual "stay away from drugs" message but couched it in a way that wasn't preachy or pompous. He seemed to like the sound of his own voice, but I couldn't blame him. He was so sincere, I began to feel guilty about this not being a real interview. The bottom line was that after listening to him talk, I found him incredibly likable. I had to keep reminding myself that he had betrayed Dulcie.

Close to half an hour later, he asked if he'd given us enough. Luke and I stood and thanked him. He reached across the desk and shook each of our hands. "It's been a pleasure," Professor Brown said. "Please send me a copy of the article. I'd love to show it to my own students."

I felt my stomach fall to my toes, but I assured him we would.

Once we were back on the street, I sneaked a look at Luke. Night had fallen, and the streets were crowded with college kids.

"What do you think?" I asked him.

"He's hiding something," Luke stated without a hint of doubt.

"Do you think he was worried about Dulcie's memoir? Do you think he was afraid she might reveal something about him?"

"I do," Luke said. "The question is, was he worried enough to kill her to keep her quiet?"

I paused at the corner under a streetlamp. "Listen, I'm calling McGrath tomorrow. It may not do any good, but it may get him back to thinking about Dulcie, if he isn't already."

"What are you going to tell him?"

"That he should be talking to the people we're talking to. That Dulcie wasn't in a frame of mind to kill herself. She was clean and having someone over for dinner, and that doesn't add up. We can leave the neighbor out of it, but both Rosetta and Lincoln should be talking to the police, not to us."

Luke thought it over. "Okay. You're right. Wanna share a cab, Watson?"

"Only if—"

"Only if you pay half," he finished, looping his arm through mine. "I know."

"You use your powers of deduction well, Mr. Holmes," I joked. But it sounded flat. All I could think of was how good it felt having him so close. Luckily, he didn't seem to notice. We walked arms linked, leaning against each other until we found a taxi.

CHaPTEr TWENTY-THree

The next morning, I called McGrath the minute I got into work. Luckily, Rona wasn't in yet, so I could use her phone without being watched and judged. But the policeman who answered told me McGrath wouldn't be in until one, so I left a message with Good Music's number.

Then I made another call. One that I'd been dreading.

I hadn't had lunch with Bernie since I broke the news to him about Dulcie's death. Marla had called me to tell me that he wasn't feeling well and that he wasn't coming in to the office for a few days. I hadn't minded; I'd needed some time off from my uncle after what I'd discovered about his shady dealings with Dulcie. But now I had to clear the air between us and get some straight answers. We set up lunch at The Turf.

WHEN I SPOTTED BERNIE at our usual table, I was surprised at how tired he looked. He seemed to have lost some weight. His tan face was pasty. Something about him had changed.

His sadness was almost palpable. He'd already ordered a drink, and it was half gone, even though I was only a minute late.

"How's it going, Justice, baby?" he asked as I sat down. "Writing any smashes?"

"I've written one song I like a lot," I told him. "Are you okay, Uncle Bernie?"

"Fine," he said, downing the rest of his stinger in one gulp. "What does Bobby think of your song?"

"He hasn't heard it yet. I'm saving it until just the right artist is looking."

Bernie nodded, rattling the ice cubes. "Good plan. Nothing older than yesterday's song except yesterday's news." There was a silence as he motioned for another drink.

I struggled to find a way to ask my question. "Uncle Bernie, I have something on my mind, and I don't know quite how to say it."

"Well," said Bernie with a little bit of his old twinkle, "I'll tell you how to say it once you tell me what it is."

"Very funny." I tried to match his light tone but couldn't. "This is serious." I took a ragged breath. "I need to know if you put your name on songs you didn't write. Specifically on songs written by Dulcie Brown."

He blinked a few times at me, waiting for the waiter to return with his next stinger. Then he shrugged. "The short answer is yes."

My jaw tightened. "Please, if there's a long answer, I want to hear it."

"Justice, baby, I can see you're upset. You have the same

look on your face Janny gets." He managed a sad chuckle. "But you're still a kid. There's a lot you don't know. I found Dulcie Brown when she was nowhere, and I took her somewhere. She had the talent, but I had the smarts, and without me and George, she would have slipped into oblivion like hundreds—no, thousands—of good-looking colored girls who can sing."

"And that excuses you?" I returned, a little too loudly. The waiter brought his drink.

Bernie glanced around and took another sip of his stinger. He lowered his voice. "You gotta understand, this is the music *business*. Why do you think I take you to lunch? Why do you think I'm trying to teach you everything I know? You have writing talent, but I had another kind. I took artists who didn't know what they were doing or how to do it, and I invested my time and money in them. I had to find a way of sharing in their success."

I shook my head, trying to keep the disgust out of my voice. "But you were their manager and their publisher—and sometimes even their record producer and record company. So you got your own royalty. Why did you have to take theirs, too?"

Bernie sighed. "Funny. I guess I really forgot that you're just a kid. You're too naïve to understand."

"So explain it to me."

His eyes hardened. "It wasn't enough considering the investment I made." He spoke coolly and crisply now, as if I were a business associate. He pulled out a gold toothpick and stuck it between his teeth. "I bet on the song," he said as he chewed it. "The song is what lives on. After the records stop selling and the singer stops touring, people keep recording a hit song. It lasts a few lifetimes. I needed to be part of those hits forever. Make sense?"

"What do you mean, 'needed'?" I leaned across the menu I hadn't bothered to open. "Uncle Bernie, you *wanted* to be a bigger part of those songs than you deserved to be. You bet on *people* who knew you and trusted you, not horses."

The waiter appeared again, eager to take our order.

"In a minute," Bernie snapped at him. He turned back to me. "Things are changing now, but everybody did it back then. It was the way the business worked. Justice, baby, you gotta grow up and smell the money. Damn it, I did deserve it. I created the person who created the song. Don't you get that?"

"No, I don't." I backed off a bit and found myself in a strange state of calm. "What I get is that you stole. And you knew it was wrong because you covered it up. You kept two sets of books. I know all about it. You took advantage of people who didn't know how music publishing worked or were so desperate that they'd do anything to get a break. So desperate they'd even give away something that was rightfully theirs."

Bernie spit the toothpick back into his hand and dropped it back into the cylinder, avoiding my eyes. "It really hurts me to hear this," he said under his breath. "That you of all people should hurl these accusations at me disturbs me beyond words. JJ, I want you to understand. I had great affection for all my artists. Dulcie Brown was . . ." He stopped.

"Was what, Uncle Bernie?"

"She was special." His voice trembled. "Don't think I didn't care about her. I still haven't gotten over her suicide."

"Neither have I," I told him.

He stared down at the ice cubes in his empty glass. "I don't know what else to say to you, Justice, baby, except that I care about you, too."

"Does that mean you want to put your name on my songs, too?" I blurted out.

His head snapped up. The grimace on his face told me I had gone too far. His expression shifted from sadness to rage.

"I'm sorry, Uncle Bernie. I didn't mean that—"

"Justice," he cut in, his teeth clenched, "if you were anyone else, I'd walk away from this table. But I have a feeling that this is about something more than my business practices. So why don't you say what's really on your mind?"

I looked into his eyes, trying to read what was behind them, wishing I'd held back more. "I'm sorry," I said again. "But you're right. You've been so unavailable and upset since Dulcie's death, I can't help but wonder if there is something about your relationship with her that you're hiding."

He turned away and snapped his fingers for the waiter. "Is this about how a one-hit wonder became a janitor in our building? Is that what's eating you? You're out of your league here, Justice, baby. You've lived a very sheltered life. Dulcie was a client and a friend years ago before you were even born. Her death shook me. And I do have a heart, no matter what you or your mother may think."

"I know you do, Uncle Bernie." I stood and pushed back my chair as the waiter approached. "I've seen it. And I love you. But now I've lost someone who was hurt by the way you operate. So I'd like to take a break from our lunches for a while."

Bernie didn't react. He showed no emotion other than impatience for his next vodka stinger. For the first time in my life I understood what the term *poker face* meant. He didn't even blink. "For a while or for good?" he asked.

"I don't know," I said. My voice cracked. "For good, for now. I gotta go."

Only then did his face fall.

I turned and walked away. I knew then for sure Bernie hadn't been conning me. And I hadn't been conning him either. He did have a heart. I only wondered if it was hurting as much as mine was.

CHAPTER TWENTY-FOUR

I held in the tears until I got into the elevator, but all Nick had to say was "What's wrong, kiddo?" for the floodgates to open the way they typically did in his "office." He stopped between floors and let me cry it out. As polite as ever, he just stood there with a solemn face until my hand-kerchief was a soggy mess, then handed me a Kleenex.

"Do you want to talk?" he asked.

"I don't know." I answered. But I did want to talk, and he sensed it. "Nick, what do you do when someone you love disappoints you? When they do stuff that breaks your heart? Do you forget that you love them? Do you get over it?"

"That happens to be a subject I know all about," Nick answered without hesitation. He closed his eyes for a moment, reaching back into his memory. "It happened when I was just a little kid, but it feels like yesterday."

I sniffed and leaned against the elevator wall. "Can you tell me about it?"

"Sure." He adjusted his cap and looked down at his shiny shoes. "It was my mother. When I was ten, my ma told my pop that she wanted to 'find herself.' Turns out she was 'finding herself' with her English-as-a-second-language teacher. I found that out later. But the next night, Ma told me she was leaving us. When she told me she was going away, I felt . . . I can't even tell you how I felt. It was like I was dying. She was standing there with her suitcase, and I grabbed at her skirt. And she said . . . I'll never forget her words . . ." He tried to repeat them, but even after all these years he couldn't. He shook his head.

"I'm so sorry," I breathed. "I shouldn't have asked. It's so much worse than what happened to me."

He shrugged and straightened. "Everyone's pain is their own. That's one thing I've learned. You can't compare pain."

"I'm just sorry I made you remember that," I said.

"That's okay, kiddo," Nick said softly. "The doctor's office is closed now." He put on his cheery face and started the elevator. Then he stopped for a second and smiled at me with genuine affection. "Just be strong and let it go. It's all you can ever do."

AFTER WORK I HEADED down to 717 to fill Luke in on my lunch with Bernie. The story that came pouring out was an incoherent jumble. I covered the facts we knew, Bernie's rationalizations, my reactions, and my contradictory feelings, loving him and hating him. As usual Luke listened, hanging on to every word of what would have sounded to anyone else like gibberish.

No one ever understood me quite the way Luke did. Loving someone whose ethics you hated was one of our bonds. He and his dad were mirror images of my uncle and me. Luke and I were both struggling to come to terms with our feelings. But even so, I knew I had it easier. He needed to find peace within himself since he could never make peace with his father. I still had a chance with Bernie.

"Listen, JJ, I honestly believe your relationship with Bernie will find its way," Luke said, sitting beside me on the sofa. "Just don't push it right now."

"You're right," I said. "I need to let go. Get my mind on something else."

"I've got something that could help." He hopped up and grabbed a piece of notebook paper from the desk and handed it to me. "Tell me what you think. Be honest. It's called 'Something Like a Miracle.' I mean . . . unless you think of something better."

I nodded, gripping the paper tightly.

There I was, drowning in my own tears,
Fighting my old, familiar fears,
Feeling as wasted as all my wasted years,
And looking in my eyes, I came to realize
I needed something like a miracle,
And my miracle was overdue.
I needed someone who could heal my soul,
Someone to make my broken heart feel whole.
I needed something like a miracle to get me through.
I needed someone just like you.

My hands trembled as I read the lines, once, twice, three times. I loved every word. I loved that it was more than the *I love you; why don't you love me* type of songs that Bobby liked. I loved that it was about a deeper love, a love that could bring salvation to someone whose spirit was broken. I tried not to let myself wonder if this song was also autobiographical, if the "you" scrawled on the paper was the "me" sitting across from him.

But it had to be, right? I was drawn to Luke in so many ways—emotionally, physically, and creatively. There was a cloud of sadness over him that I wanted to lift. I was never happier than when I was making him smile, but I had no idea if he felt anything more than a growing friendship toward me. He'd never made any kind of move beyond the gentlemanly kind. Maybe we were just pals. If that was how he felt, I'd have to accept it.

"Are you going to tell me what you think?" he blurted out.

I took a second to collect myself. Best just to focus on the real possibilities. "It's . . . um, extraordinary. It's inspirational. Will you let me try to write to it?"

"That's why you're holding it. I was hoping you'd want to. Listen, tonight is my last night in the apartment. We have a Bösendorfer there. I'd love to hear you play it."

"A real Bösendorfer?" I gasped. I knew I sounded like the biggest music nerd in the world, but it was enough to get a smile out of him. "Are you kidding? I would love the chance to hear what one sounds like."

He jerked his head toward the door. "Come on, then. I know you turn into a pumpkin bagel at eleven."

CHAPTER TWENTY-FIVE

After a short bus ride and a walk, we arrived at 67th Street and Park Avenue, one of the swankiest blocks in the city. A white-gloved doorman opened the door for us, and we rode up to the fifteenth floor in an oak-paneled car, operated by a uniformed elevator man. I really felt as if I was in Oz when the elevator opened right into the apartment. I had only seen that in movies.

I looked around in awed silence, trying to wrap my head around the fact that Luke lived here—or at least that he would until tomorrow morning. The rooms were huge, the ceilings were high, the walls were adorned with intricate moldings and the furnishings were as elegant as any I'd ever seen. But there were no boxes. All the books and knickknacks were still on the shelves.

"This is your last night?" I asked turning to Luke. "Give it to me straight; you brought me here to pack, didn't you?"

He laughed quietly. "The buyer purchased it fully

furnished. I just have to grab my suitcase. I never was attached to all this stuff, and now somehow it all feels tainted."

I shook my head. "But this was your home."

"Not really. Dad sent me to Eaglebrook in seventh grade." He paused when he caught my baffled look. "It's a boarding school. I can't blame him; he was my only parent, and his job was his life. Besides, it wasn't that bad. From there I went to Hotchkiss, another boarding school. I'm supposed to go to Princeton next year, but . . ."

"But what?" I asked. Mostly I was thinking, *Princeton is close. New Jersey is just across the river. A train ride away.*

"But I'm not sure what I'm going to do. I mean, now that I know what Dad was really up to and the truth about my past."

I nodded. It was the first time he'd even acknowledged to me that his race might affect his future. I really wanted to know what his feelings were about that, but I also knew that he wasn't ready to share them yet.

"I was thinking of taking a break . . ." He looked up with that half-smile that always made me want more. "Why are we even talking about this? I brought you here to play our Bösendorfer."

Before I could protest, he waved for me to follow him and vanished around a corner. There, in another lavish living room—the music room, I guess—was the most gorgeous grand piano I'd ever seen, long and ebony, its black curves gleaming. I made a beeline for it, easing myself onto the bench, my eyes hungrily roving over the keys. I'd read about its warm rich tone, and of course I'd heard it on records. I knew about the geniuses that played and swore by it, like George Gershwin.

Reaching back into my musical memory, I managed to recall Gershwin's "Rhapsody in Blue," a piece I'd learned when I was still taking lessons. I played as much as I could remember. The piano's tone was everything I imagined it would be. It sounded like the light in the room: warm, rich, and perfect. It even made me sound like a better pianist than I was.

When I glanced up, Luke was sitting next to me. I hadn't even noticed. I lowered my eyes, my pulse picking up a notch.

"I love that you played that," he said. "Believe it or not, my dad was nuts about Gershwin. It was a part of him that I love to remember."

"Do you have the lyrics to 'Something Like a Miracle'?" I asked.

The Bösendorfer had stirred something in me, and I didn't want to lose the inspiration. Luke pulled the folded paper from his pocket and slid it onto the piano's music stand. I groped around for a while, but it didn't take long to find a melody—Gershwinesque in its blues notes and jazz changes, but pop, too. When I'd repeated it a few times, Luke began to sing with me. *"I needed something like a miracle to get me through / I needed someone just like you."*

We sang the chorus over and over, both laughing out loud just because it sounded so good. When I stopped, we sighed in unison.

The seconds ticked by. If I could have frozen myself

there—in that place, in that moment, with the connection I had to this boy—I would have done it in an instant.

"The lyrics are about you, you know," Luke said out of the blue. "You saved my life. I have never met anyone like you."

My knees turned to jelly under the keyboard. Was I imagining things in my desire to make everything perfect with Luke? No, I wasn't. Everything always fit somehow when it was the two of us. He'd said the words I'd prayed he'd say. My head fell to his shoulder. I'm not even sure I'd thought to put it there.

"Thank you," I whispered. "Please don't think I'm unoriginal if I tell you I feel the same way about you." I squeezed my eyes shut, trying to reconcile the sudden and overwhelming joy I felt with the fear that crept in. "Where are you going tomorrow? Where will you be living?"

He laughed softly, his breath nuzzling my forehead. "Well, to describe my new place generously, it's a crummy basement apartment in a brownstone in Greenwich Village."

"But why are you moving into someplace like that when you must have sold this place for a fortune?"

Luke sat up straight, so that I had to take my head off his shoulder. He took my hands in his. His cat eyes bored into mine, and he spoke with an intensity I'd never heard before. "I did. But JJ, I have to live my way now. No matter what happens, I'll be okay. I'm going to use that money to pay back the people my father ripped off. At least as many as I can. It's the only way I can live with myself. In the meantime, I got a part-time job at Sam Goody's. I'll be selling records until I figure out whether I'm going to college in the fall. I don't know yet. Like I said, I might be taking some time off."

I searched those glorious green eyes for hope. "Maybe we'll get a song recorded, and you won't have to do that for long. When we finish this one, we'll have two songs for Bobby to pitch. Maybe we can be real songwriters who earn a living at it."

He shrugged. "That would be nice. But JJ, you know what's out there. So much on the radio is crap . . ." Only then did his eyes brighten. "You know there's a guy who plays and sings down in the village who just put out a new album I want you to hear. His songs really say something. I don't know if we'll be able to find singers who want to record songs that say something, but we could try."

I thought of Bobby and his obsession with the charts. "We could try," I echoed.

Luke started to slide away from me. Instinctively I reached out to grab his arm, to keep him there, to keep him right next to me.

"What's the name of the album?" I asked, trying to cover for how I'd pounced. "I want to get it."

"It's called *The Freewheelin' Bob Dylan.* Trust me, you'll like it a lot."

"I'm sure I will," I whispered. "I trust you. But let's stop second-guessing the future. Let's just work on our songs together. Let's just . . . be together."

At first I was terrified I'd said too much.

He didn't respond. Without warning, he leaned forward and kissed me softly on the lips. He tasted like Dr. Brown's cream soda, and sweetness, and every possible wonderful thing I could imagine. His lips were like velvet. I kissed him back. I'd never really kissed a boy before, not in any way that meant anything. I let him take over.

I'm not sure how long we made out on that piano bench. All I know was that the clock was striking eleven when I walked through the front door of our silent apartment. My family was fast asleep. I knew that I would replay tonight a hundred times in my head before I joined them in the morning.

CHaPTeR TWeNTY-SIX

I don't know why, but the next day, even though I put on an outfit I'd worn many times before, I felt beautiful. When I got to work, I floated into the copy room to find Rona waiting for me.

"What new slavish chore do you have for me, mistress?" I cracked.

But Rona didn't smile back. "I just want to give you a little advice," she said seriously. "Bobby isn't happy that you haven't played any songs for him. He knows about the studio time I booked for you."

The dreamy feeling faded. I looked at her, unsure of what to say.

"I'm on your side, JJ," she said, pulling me close. She lowered her voice to make sure nobody overheard. "I've got a feeling you've got a guy or something that's distracting you. Sometimes you're not all here. I just want the boss to know you're doing the songwriting he expects you to do. You have a contract, remember?"

I nodded, the bliss now escaping from my body as if I'd sprung a happiness leak. "I . . . okay. I get it. Thanks, Ro."

"That's what friends are for," she replied as she headed for the door.

"That sounds like a song title," I muttered.

"Oh, please," she scoffed. "Bobby wants love songs, not friend songs. Oh, by the way, you got two calls. Marla Rubin and a Detective Frank McGrath." She paused and turned to me, sympathy in her eyes. "You can use the phone at my desk when I take my lunch break, okay?"

"More than okay," I responded sheepishly. "Thanks."

I called Marla as soon as Rona took off. The office was deserted at lunchtime. She picked up on the second ring.

"Hello?" she sniffled hoarsely. I barely recognized her voice.

"Marla? It's JJ Green. Are you okay?"

"JJ, I'm so glad you called." She let out a shaky sigh. "Bernie's a mess. He's so sad about the way things ended between you yesterday. I've never seen him like this, sweetheart. He doesn't even want to go in to the office. It's scaring me. Please, just come for dinner so you two can continue to talk."

I stood there, clutching the phone and staring at Bobby Goodman's closed door, a bad feeling in my gut. In all my delirium over Luke, I'd never considered that Bernie might actually be hurt that I'd walked out on him. I'd seen his face; I knew he cared, but I'd just assumed he'd go on with life, taking bets and making money. I wasn't ready to see him, but there was no way I could refuse Marla. She was begging me on behalf of someone she loved.

"Listen, Marla, you knew George Silver, right?" I asked.

"Of course. He and Bernie were partners for years. We were so sorry when he finally passed away." She sniffled again. "Why do you ask?"

"I met his son, and we became friends. He's been here in the building a lot, cleaning out his dad's office. Could I bring him to dinner?"

The idea hadn't even fully formed until I posed the question. But Luke deserved to hear the truth from his father's former partner, too. He deserved to hear whatever Uncle Bernie knew about his mother as well. Bernie was complicit in the cover-up. He could have told Luke the truth any time. And I guess I felt I needed support facing Bernie again. There was no better support than Luke.

"Of course you can bring him," Marla said. "Bernie hasn't seen him since George's memorial service. Tonight at seven, okay?"

"Okay." I answered as cheerfully as I could. But familiar dread crept back over me—dread of plunging once more into that unresolved conversation about ethics, morals, and music business behavior. And it wasn't as if I were exactly blameless either. Janny still didn't know about my secret relationship with Bernie and Marla. None of the Greens did. If I were completely honest with myself, it hadn't weighed very heavily on my conscience. Mostly I'd been focused on proving them wrong. Now I had another secret relationship, too—another relationship I wasn't ready to share with anyone. Not until Luke figured out for himself how he was going to address his past and who he really was.

I dropped the phone on the hook, then dialed the phone number Rona had left me for Frank McGrath. It must have been some sort of private number because nobody answered. After ten rings, I hung up. Honestly, I was relieved. With Rona's warning about Bobby and my guilt over Uncle Bernie, I wasn't sure if I could handle whatever news Detective McGrath wanted to tell me. Besides, chances were I couldn't answer the questions he wanted to ask.

I needed a break from Dulcie Brown's death. The problem was every single part of my life was tied to it.

LUKE HAD SPENT THE day moving into his new apartment. When I'd finally disentangled myself from his arms the previous night, we'd agreed to meet at his dad's office at 6 p.m. Needless to say, I'd been hoping for another long night of being back in those arms. I could tell that he felt the same way. At the very least, he couldn't hide that he wasn't thrilled about a surprise dinner at Uncle Bernie's. But he understood both why I needed to go and why I'd invited him.

"Lucky for Uncle Bernie, I showered and changed to impress you," he joked quietly.

He did look devastatingly handsome, his tight curls wet and combed. He wore a tweed blazer, a pressed shirt, and a skinny black tie. We didn't say much after we left the building beyond muttering relief that Antonio was our elevator man on the way down. Neither of us was in the mood for Nick's chatter or questions. We walked the few blocks to Bernie and Marla's apartment holding hands. It felt like the most natural thing in the world; a few people even smiled our way to see young love in bloom.

Then I thought of Dulcie and George walking together through hostile streets. I couldn't help but wonder if we would be on the receiving end of that same hatred if Luke looked more like his mother.

UNCLE BERNIE GREETED ME with a bear hug and Luke with a warm embrace. "So my favorite teenagers found each other. I can't tell you how happy that makes me."

I wasn't sure if he sensed the truth, or if he just figured we were friends. It seemed like the former, which made me nervous. Marla fluttered around, making sure we were all comfortable, bringing Bernie a martini and Luke and me Cokes. I could see how relieved she was that we were there. I didn't want this to turn out bad for her. I wanted to get any bad part of the discussion over and done before dinner.

"Uncle Bernie, I wonder if you can tell me something about Dulcie?" I asked quietly, once we were all sitting down.

He took a sip of his drink. "Depends what it is, Justice, baby."

"When I was working with her, she wore a really beautiful necklace. It was a gold note on a chain. She told me it was a gift from a friend. She was going to ask her friend where they got it, but then . . ." My voice faded, then picked up. "I know you hadn't seen her in a while, but I wondered if she wore it when you and George managed her. I guess I just want to know if you knew where it came from?"

"I'm not exactly the kind of guy who notices women's jewelry unless I give it to them," Bernie pointed out, smiling at Marla. "I have no idea if Dulcie Brown wore a necklace."

I nodded. "It just struck me that it looked a bit like Marla's diamond musical note, so I thought I'd ask."

"Everybody in the music biz gives their girlfriend a music note of some kind," Marla chimed in proudly. "But not many have one as gorgeous as mine."

"Keep that in mind, Luke," Bernie said with a wink. "I'll remind you when JJ's birthday comes around."

I was so embarrassed and flustered that I lost my train of thought. Time to change the subject. "What's for dinner?" I asked. "I'm starved."

But before we could even get up, the doorbell rang.

"Who else did you invite, babe?" Bernie asked Marla.

"Not a soul," she replied, puzzled. She stood and headed for the door. We all peered after her.

To everyone's surprise, she returned an instant later accompanied by Detective Frank McGrath and another uniformed cop. A fleeting shadow passed over Bernie's face, but he quickly covered it with one of his winning grins. He was a master of the grin.

"Hey, Frank, what's going on?" he said amiably. "Got no place to go for dinner?"

Frank acknowledged me with a nod and turned his attention to Bernie. "Sorry to disturb your get-together, Bernie, but I have to ask you to come downtown with me."

"And why is that, may I ask?" Marla asked curtly.

"Mr. Rubin's name has come up in an investigation involving the illegal promotion of records," McGrath said as the other cop moved toward Uncle Bernie. "We have some questions to ask him. Unfortunately, they can't wait."

"What else is new?" Bernie wanted to know. He stood up.

"Do you want me to come with you?" Luke asked. "Maybe I can help."

Bernie smiled at him. "You wanna help? Stay here with Marla, see she doesn't run out of tissues and help finish off that roast she slaved over."

I glanced at Marla. Sure enough, she'd already begun to sob silently.

Bernie sidestepped the second cop and slipped his arm through McGrath's. "'Round up the usual suspects,'" he quoted from *Casablanca*, his favorite movie. "No hard feelings, Frank. I understand. It's what they pay you for."

Marla lurched over and threw her arms around her husband, tossing McGrath a dirty look. "Just remember, Detective," she said, "this man has a family waiting for him."

"Don't worry, babe," Bernie told her. "I'll be back before dessert."

CHAPTER TWENTY-SEVEN

We sat in the living room silently for ten awful endless minutes—Marla, Luke, and me. At least Marla had finally stopped crying. Then she suggested we go in and start on the salad, because Bernie never liked salad.

"Does anyone want to bet on whether he'll *really* be back in time for dessert?" she asked, almost setting off her own tears again.

Luke and I looked at each other. We hadn't signed up for this, but there was no way out. Marla ushered us into the dining room, and we plodded after her, taking our seats. She began to dole out the salad from a large crystal bowl.

The conversation that followed was supremely uncomfortable, and yet in some way I got to know Marla better in those forty-five minutes than in all the time since we'd met. She spilled everything. How she could never get used to Bernie being hauled in by the police for some illegal action, even though they could never make anything stick. How she had to get used to being regarded as a trophy wife, who had maried for money, even though the truth was that she was madly in love with him. How her father had died when she was very young, and she'd never had a reliable man in her life until Bernie.

I tried not to squirm. She was totally charmed by his music biz smarts. Even his underhanded behavior was seductive to her. I guess when you love someone, you see them as who you want them to be. She saw Bernie as a sexy, lovable rogue. She was still wowed by his good looks. It was clear Bernie was both a father figure as well as a husband to her, although she didn't seem to realize it.

The phone rang. Marla ran to get it.

I breathed a sigh of relief. I was afraid that Marla's rant might be taking us into more graphic details about her attraction to my uncle.

Luke leaned toward me. "Don't be embarrassed," he whispered. "George got hauled down a few times. It's part of who they are, or in George's case, who he was."

"What?" Marla shrieked from the other room. "This is crazy! They can't do this to you!"

Luke's eyes met mine again. We both dropped our silverware onto our plates and pushed back from the table, but Marla was already storming back into the dining room. Her face was ashen. She had a hard time walking to a chair to sit down.

"What is it?" I asked. "Did something happen to Bernie?"

She just sat there without saying a word, almost as if she were in shock.

"Marla?" I took her hand and kneeled next to her. "Tell me what happened."

After a few seconds, she turned to me and spoke in a choked voice. "The payola thing was just a trick to get Bernie to go with them. When they got down there, they started questioning him about Dulcie Brown's death."

Oh, my God. I felt a stab of guilt. Was this my fault somehow? Had my call pushed McGrath into homicide mode? Was Bernie paying the price of my meddling? Or was this only the way to find out the truth? The guilt grew, but wasn't the truth what I wanted, no matter where it would take me?

"But he hadn't seen her in years," I murmured, answering my own unspoken question.

"What exactly do the police have on him?" Luke asked Marla.

She buried her mascara-stained face in her hands for a minute, then looked up. "The painters working for the new tenant came across a gold toothpick that they turned over to the police. Bernie and those stupid toothpicks. The cops want to know how it got there. He used his one phone call to tell me to call his lawyer." Marla stood up on shaky legs. "I can't even think of the guy's name," she whispered.

"What kind of lawyer is he?" I asked.

"I don't know," Marla murmured in a daze. "A music business lawyer, I guess." All of a sudden she turned to me, her face twisted in anger and sadness. "JJ, how could Bernie's toothpick show up in that woman's apartment? He told us he hadn't seen her in years."

I tried my best to sound calm, even though my heart was beating double-time. "I'm sure there's an explanation, and he'll give it to us. But right now Bernie doesn't need a music lawyer. He needs a criminal attorney. I glanced at Luke. "I hate to do this but would you mind staying with her?"

"I was going to offer anyway," he answered. "Is that all right with you, Mrs. Rubin? I'd prefer you not be alone right now, and I know it would make JJ feel better."

She nodded vacantly. I wondered if she'd even heard him. Luke gently led her back into the living room. I wanted to sweep him into my arms. I owed him for this and so much more. But I would have to thank him later.

I flew out of the door, and less than a minute later, was in a taxi and headed for home. Bernie was many things, but he was no murderer. With my mom's help, we'd prove it.

IN THE SHORT TIME it took to get home, my resolve to recruit Janny to represent the brother she'd disowned had almost melted away completely. I kept picturing her enraged reaction, her disgust at yet another secret I'd kept from her, that harsh and dismissive voice. I was so nervous, I almost couldn't open my own front door. My hands were clammy and trembling. On my third try, the key finally clicked in the lock. There was laughter coming from the dining room. I headed for it to find Jeff and Janny having dinner.

My mother's face broke into a wide smile. "JJ, how wonderful to see you. You haven't been home for dinner in what seems like forever. Take Dad's place. He'll be back in time for dessert."

There was no time for gentle lead-ins, so I just came out

with it. "Mom," I said, "I have something to tell you. I've spent some time with Uncle Bernie this summer."

Janny's eyes turned to steel. She threw her napkin on her plate. "I knew it." She groaned.

"Please," I continued, "before you get upset and start scolding me, just let me finish. He's been very kind to me, but now he's in a jam. Something awful has happened, and he needs your help."

Janny's face registered zero sympathy. "Something awful always seems to happen to Bernie," she stated. "He creates awful. It's his specialty."

"Please, Mom." The words lodged in my throat. "He's been arrested. The police think he's involved in a murder. Your friend Frank McGrath is working the case."

"Holy crap," Jeff muttered.

My mother shot him a glare. She turned to me and paused as she struggled to find the words she needed. "I understand," she said. "He's got you all involved, Justice. It's what he does. He sucks people into his vortex and then destroys them. I vowed I'd never let him do that to my family or me. So you'll understand if I insist that he let him get himself out of whatever he's gotten into."

Unbelievable, I thought. If only she could see herself. She the one who was always spouting clichés, like "ninety percent of the law is compassion." It was so hypocritical. I knew I had to pull out all the stops, even if it meant a low blow. "Is that what you think Grandma and Grandpa would have wanted you to do?" I asked, my voice rising. "Would they have wanted you to desert your brother when he needed you most?"

"This topic is closed," Janny retorted. "Now if you—"

"JJ has a point, Mom," Jeffrey interrupted quietly. "He's your *brother*."

Janny and I both stared at him.

Every now and then—about as often as, say, a total eclipse of the sun—my brother will demonstrate that he's something more than a brown-nosing schmuck who lives for getting the best of me. Then again, revealing one's true self, or at least another side of one's self, seemed to be a recent recurring theme in my life.

My mother looked so distraught that for a moment, I felt a twinge of regret. Keeping Bernie out of her life was almost a religious commitment. Finally she stood up and smoothed the skirt of her navy sheath dress. "You're right, JJ," she said. Once again, her voice was calm and professional. She had shifted into lawyer mode. "Both of you are right. I know neither of you would abandon the other in a time of need. Jeffrey, please get my purse and jacket. They're in the bedroom."

My brother nodded and scooted out of the dining room.

Janny leveled her gaze at me. "I don't have a good feeling about this," she said softly, "but you made your point very well."

"Thanks," I said. There wasn't anything more to add. I followed her into the hall.

The front door opened, and Jules walked in, his face weary from the New York heat and a full day in court. When he saw me, he perked up. "JJ! What a treat. What brings you here before eleven?"

"She came here to tell us about Bernie," Janny explained without any preliminaries. "He's in police custody."

"What else is new?" Jules asked with a chuckle.

"It's not funny, Jules," she snapped. "They think maybe he killed somebody."

Jeff arrived and handed over her jacket and purse.

Jules rubbed his chin. "I see," he said after a moment. It seemed he'd snapped into legal mode, too. Then he laid a hand on Janny's arm in as intimate a way as I'd ever seen. "Did he?"

"I don't know," Janny replied, her voice fragile. "All I know is that he needs me."

CHAPTER TWENTY-EIGHT

I headed back to Bernie's apartment while Janny raced to catch a cab down to the police station. When I rang the bell, Luke opened the door and put a finger to his lips. Marla had fallen asleep on the couch, no doubt trying to escape the horrible reality of her situation. All five feet ten of her was curled up into a fetal position. She had cried off all her eye makeup. Right now, she almost looked like a little kid.

Before I could whisper an apology to Luke for dragging him into this mess tonight, he kissed me. I kissed him back. Then we sat down across from Marla in silence.

An hour later, we finally heard a key turning in the door. When it opened, Marla was startled back into consciousness. At the sight of Bernie, she flew off the sofa and into his arms and covered his face with kisses.

"Calm down, babe," he murmured with a gravelly laugh. "Everything's okay."

We stood there awkwardly for a moment. Janny appeared

behind him, zeroed in on me, and waved me toward the door. She didn't even seem to see Luke. Maybe she just didn't want to be bothered with any more surprises.

Bernie unwrapped Marla's arms and turned to his sister. "My wife, Marla; my sister, Janice Green," he explained. "I can't thank you enough for getting me out of there, Janny. I owe you. You, too, Justice, baby."

"Anyone could have done it," Janny demurred. "JJ could have gotten you out herself. They didn't have enough to hold you. They're just flailing around, looking for a suspect. They hoped they could keep you talking until you incriminated yourself." She strode toward the door. "You're innocent, so you'll be fine. You hadn't even seen this woman in years, correct?" Her eyes flashed back to me. "We'll be going now. Call me if you need me."

"Wait," Bernie said.

Janny paused at the door and sighed dramatically. "Yes?"

"I have . . . I have something to say, and you all need to hear it." Bernie sat down in an armchair and rubbed his temples. He winced for a second, as if hit by an invisible fist, then waved us over. "Please sit down. It'll just take a few minutes."

My heart thudded. This was bad. I could feel it. I settled in on the couch next to Luke. Janny remained standing, of course. Marla sat on the armchair across from Bernie.

His gaze swept over all of us. "Janny, this matter isn't over yet. I think I may be calling on you again." I'd never heard him sound so weak or vulnerable. He turned to Marla. "Marla, I love you with all my heart, but I haven't been honest with you. I . . . I'd been seeing

Dulcie Brown. I was having a relationship with her. It was so wrong, and I am so sorry."

Marla's lips pressed into a tight line. Luke and I sat there, stunned and embarrassed. "Tell me the whole story, Bernard," Marla demanded. "Don't leave anything out on anyone's account."

Bernie walked puposefully over to his wife. "I ran into her going into the Brill Building a year or so ago. She was applying for a custodial job. I helped her get it. I felt in some way I had to make up for abandoning her when she had her drug problem. I was the one who pushed George to drop her later. It always preyed on me. Something about her got to me . . . I don't know. Maybe I confused pity with affection. I'm sorry, Marla."

Marla's eyes were brimming but she held back the tears. She stood up and faced him down, seeming to tower over him, her back ramrod straight. "Do you screw everyone you feel sorry for, Bernard?"

His shoulders sagged. "Babe, you have every right to be furious, but I'm begging you to forgive me. I'll spend the rest of my life making it up to you. Just give me that chance."

I cringed, horrified but unable to look away. All I could think was, *I'm never inviting Luke to a family dinner again.*

Bernie's eyes grew moist. "I swear, baby, I was going to end it."

"By killing her?" she demanded.

"My God, of course not," he gasped. He looked up, searching her eyes. "I had nothing to do with that. I realized I couldn't go on with it. The guilt was unbearable."

When Bernie actually got down on his knees in front of her, I could feel my face turning red. I was beyond mortified for the both of them. Grown-ups should not behave this way.

"I'm begging you to give me another chance, baby," he pleaded. "I'll do anything you want me to do to make you trust me again."

Marla wiped the tears from her eyes with the back of her hand like a little girl. It was as if they had both forgotten that we were there. Maybe they had.

"I love you, Bernie," she whispered. "You know that. Everybody may think I'm just your status symbol wife, that I'm with you for the stuff, the money, but you're everything to me. I was crazy in love with you when I married you, and you know it."

"Are you still in love with me?" Bernie asked, his voice thick.

She nodded, unable to speak. Bernie swept her into his arms and kissed her with desperate passion. I'd never wanted so badly to disappear, get vaporized by an A-bomb or gobbled up by King Kong. Anything would have been better than sitting these two strip naked emotionally. After they broke apart, there was an endless moment of silence. Embarrassment hung in the air like the smoke from one of Bernie's Cuban cigars.

Someone had to say something, and I elected myself. "Well, Luke," I announced with as much phony perkiness as I could muster, "what better time could there be to introduce you to my mom?"

CHAPTER TWENTY-NINE

fter the shock of the previous night, it amazed me that the sun rose the next day. It appeared that life would go on. I was still haunted by the scene in Bernie's apartment, not to mention the taxi home with Janny. Excruciating was too mild a word for the interrogation; it was closer to how I imagined testifying in court. She grilled me about Bernie like the lawyer she was, prying out the truth whenever I hesitated or attempted to conceal anything. To her credit, she didn't question me about Luke. And at the end, she'd also taken my hand and held it tightly.

The last thing she said to me before bed was, "How could you be so brave and so thoughtless?"

"I learned that from you," I told her. That was the truth, too.

THE WORKDAY, WHILE SLOW torture, was uneventful. I managed to avoid Bobby. Now I was even trying to avoid Rona, who kept looking at me with a worried expression. I wondered if you could fire someone who wasn't getting paid. Then *I* began to have a worried expression. At 6 P.M. on the nose, I rode in Nick's office down to the seventh floor.

"Hey, kiddo," he said as soon as the door closed, "I've got something to run by you. Dulcie Brown's daughter came by to ask me where you worked. She wants to talk to you. I didn't tell her anything, but I got her number if you want it."

I hesitated while he opened the doors. "Thanks, Nick," I said. "You did the right thing. I'd rather call her."

Nick handed me the slip of paper with Rosetta's number.

I bounded into room 717, but before I could say a word, Luke swept me into his arms and kissed me. Once again, I tasted Dr. Brown's on his lips. I almost forgot why I was so eager to talk to him until he pulled away and saw the crumpled piece of paper in my hand.

"Rosetta Brown came by," I explained.

Before we called and arranged to meet Rosetta outside of Birdland at seven o'clock sharp, we ran through various scenarios as to why she wanted to see us after she'd been so negative. Maybe she wanted to see the memoir. Maybe she wanted to know if Dulcie had left her anything. Maybe it was something as simple as that she felt she owed us an apology.

We were not prescient in the least.

IT WAS ANOTHER HOT and sticky evening, but Rosetta emerged from Birdland looking cool and Dulcie-gorgeous in a simple sundress. Her glare was positively icy, in fact. She nodded at Luke and turned to me without so much as a hello.

"Look," she said. The sidewalk was crowded with the midtown evening rush, so she drew close to us and kept her voice down to avoid attracting attention. "I wanted to talk to you about the night my mother died. I think I should clear the air about something. After we talked, I remembered where I had seen you before. I'm willing to lay down money that you remembered where you'd seen me, too. It was at my mother's apartment building the night she died. I saw you in the crowd."

I could feel Luke's eyes on me. I nodded. "When you were up on that stage singing with tears rolling down your cheeks, I did remember seeing you there," I confessed. "I couldn't help wondering why you hadn't mentioned it."

She reached into her handbag and dug out a pack of cigarettes. Her hands trembled a little as she fumbled for a lighter. "I needed to think about it. I want to tell you now. I had gone there that evening to tell her that I was clean. I was working my twelve steps. I'm at step five. 'Admit to God and ourselves and another human being the exact nature of our wrongs.'" She clutched the lighter and cigarettes without lighting one. "I wanted that human being to be my mother. I wanted to tell her that I was wrong to blame her for my addictions. I had no one to blame but myself and to let her know . . ." She faltered. "Let her know that I forgave her."

I nodded, wanting to reach out to her. "I understand—"

"No, you don't," Rosetta insisted. "I was hoping she would say that she forgave me, too. I was hoping to get my mama back. But I never got the chance. When I got there, she was lying on the street. It hurts. It hurts a lot. If I had just gotten there earlier, maybe I could have stopped her. But you know where I was? My AA meeting. I had just shared what I was planning to do. It didn't break until six thirty."

I blinked back a tear. It was almost too tragic to bear. "It wasn't your fault," I murmured.

She shrugged. "I guess I know that deep down. There was just so much I wanted to say to her . . ." Her voice trailed off.

To Rosetta's surprise—and mine—Luke threw his arms around her in a bear hug. "I'm so relieved to know that," he half-whispered.

She pulled away with an arched eyebrow. "Don't get any ideas, white boy," she said, but her tone had softened.

"No ideas at all. Just really happy that you cleared that up, for JJ's sake."

"He's a very affectionate person," I added.

"Well, I ain't," Rosetta retorted. "Remember that. So we're good?"

"Yeah," I said. "We're good. But I did want to ask you one thing. That necklace you're wearing—can you tell me where you got it?"

She smiled for the very first time. Pain stirred inside me again; she was such a ghostly reflection of Dulcie in that brief instant. "Someone left it for me six months ago with the hostess. It was Mama for sure, though the woman didn't say who she was. I knew. It made me start thinking about my twelve steps because I think maybe she was working hers. The necklace was a way of making amends and opening a door. I should have gone to see her back then. But I wasn't strong enough. Too bad for both of us." Her tone was so resigned, so final. It was the tone of someone for whom nothing ever worked out. It seemed to me that for Rosetta Brown, constant disappointment wasn't only expected; it was accepted—without a fight or questions. She shook her head. Cigarette still unlit, she turned and walked away, no doubt hoping never to see us again.

Life had its own plans.

CHAPTER THIRTY

The next day, the papers were full of news about the nuclear test ban treaty that President Kennedy had signed with Britain and the Russians. They agreed to ban nuclear explosions in the atmosphere, space, and underwater. But they neglected to include Good Music and the Brill Building, because on that same day, Marla walked in and dropped her own nuke on me.

Just before my lunch break, Rona poked her head into the copy room to say there was someone here to see me. My first thought was that Luke had found out something new, something important, and was too excited to call. Yet when I raced out into the waiting area I was surprised not only to find Marla, but that she was an even worse mess than when I had last seen her. Her face was puffy, and she wasn't wearing makeup. Her hair was tied into a frizzy bun.

"JJ," she sniffled, "I'm sorry to break into your day, but I have to show you something."

"Come on in," I said, grabbing her by the hand. Praying

Bobby didn't spot us, I pulled her into an empty writing cubicle and sat her down beside me on a piano bench. "Is Bernie, okay?"

"For the moment, yes," she answered with a strange look on her face. "He doesn't know I found this." Straightening, she reached into her purse and pulled out a slim gold chain with a golden note hanging from it. The very same necklace I'd just seen around Rosetta's neck. The very same one I *hadn't* seen around Dulcie's on the street that night.

"Oh, my God, where did you find it?" I gasped.

"In Bernie's jacket pocket this morning," she whispered. Her voice shook. "You know, I always check before I take his stuff to the cleaners. I found it there. I knew the second I saw it that it was the necklace you were asking Bernie about, JJ. It came from the same jeweler who made mine. His stamp was on the clasp. Bernie bought Dulcie the cheap mistress version. That explains why the chain broke so easily." She shoved it back into the bag as if it were contaminated.

I felt sick to my stomach. "What are you planning to do with it, Marla?"

"What do you think I'm going to do?" she cried. "I'm going to turn it over to that Detective McGrath and tell him where I found it." She lowered her voice when she saw me cast an anxious glance toward the closed door. "I can't be an accessory to murder. As much as I love Bernie, I couldn't live with myself if I did that."

"Please, Marla," I pleaded. I took her shaky hands. "Don't go to McGrath. Please give Bernie a chance to explain how it got there. I'm sure there's an explanation. If there isn't, please let me tell my mom what's going on, so she can help him."

Marla began to cry. Her sobs were the big, heaving kind that a little kid makes when they're in despair and out of control. "I can't believe Bernie would kill someone. Since I met Bernie, I felt so safe. I turned to him for everything. He'd always tell me what to do. But I can't tell him this. I have no one to turn to now."

I put my arms around her on instinct, to try and soothe her pain—even though what she was planning to do would devastate my family. Looking back now, I realized I was compelled to console her because she wasn't just child-like; she was childish. She *demanded* comfort. The love of her life was apparently a murderer, and she was inordinately concerned with her own well-being. Marla may have been many things, but strong wasn't one of them.

"Please, Marla," I whispered, pulling away, "talk to Bernie about this before you go to the police and give me a day to talk to my mom. It won't change anything, and you can say you needed time to think. Please, I'm begging you."

She nodded. "Okay, JJ, but just a day."

I gave her a final hug. She hurried out the door. I watched her leave just to make sure nobody spotted the tall, bedraggled stranger in heels hobble out of Good Music. Once I was back in the copy room, Rona knocked to say I had a phone call.

"I'm off to lunch, so you can take it at my desk," she said.

I hoped it was Luke. It wasn't. It was the Puerto Rican lady from Dulcie's building.

She spoke quickly and didn't give her name, and she clearly did not want to linger on a call. *"Recuerdo lo que gritó Dulcie,"* she told me. *"No puedo ayudar a cómo mi siento. No trate de hacerme sienta culpable."*

My heart stopped for a second. She remembered what Dulcie had shouted. *"I can't help how I feel. Don't try to make me feel guilty."* It was exactly the kind of thing something that a woman might yell at a lover she planned to leave, or whose lover was planning to leave her. Either way, it didn't look good for my uncle.

"Gracias, señora," I said. Then I hung up and wept. No matter how much I cared about Bernie, I had to tell this to Janny and McGrath. Poor Marla. It was beginning to look as though she really would have to find someone else to take care of her.

CHAPTER THIRTY-ONE

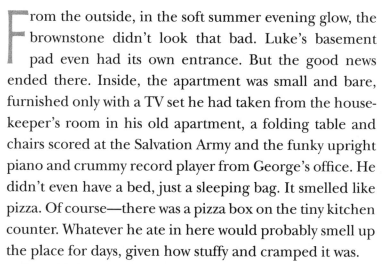

From the outside, in the soft summer evening glow, the brownstone didn't look that bad. Luke's basement pad even had its own entrance. But the good news ended there. Inside, the apartment was small and bare, furnished only with a TV set he had taken from the house-keeper's room in his old apartment, a folding table and chairs scored at the Salvation Army and the funky upright piano and crummy record player from George's office. He didn't even have a bed, just a sleeping bag. It smelled like pizza. Of course—there was a pizza box on the tiny kitchen counter. Whatever he ate in here would probably smell up the place for days, given how stuffy and cramped it was.

I couldn't imagine going from the luxury of the condo he shared with George to this. Then again, I knew the reasons, and it just made my feelings for him all the stronger. And he was in a good mood. For one, Janny had given me permission to "hang out with my friend Luke to work on songs" (my sort-of-true words) until eleven—even after I'd called her and told her everything Marla and the Puerto Rican lady had said. Maybe she suspected the truth about Luke and me and wanted to give me some freedom. More likely, she was too distracted dealing with her brother. Either way, I had four uninterrupted hours to spend with Luke in his new studio apartment.

His accountants were going through copies of George's books. He knew he would soon be paying back some of the recording artists or the heirs of those he'd ripped off. It was amazing, that this seemed to be the one thing that could make him smile: knowing that restitution would be made. When I mentioned Marla's visit and the call from the Puerto Rican lady, he agreed with me that Bernie looked guilty. He pointed out, though, that the evidence was circumstantial. Looking guilty wasn't necessarily the same as being guilty.

"Listen, before we get into all that, I want to show you something I found in George's office today." He sat me down in one of the rickety chairs and laid an official-looking document on the folding table. My eyes bulged. It was his real birth certificate. And there, with a New York State seal, in official language, were the words that left no doubt: Luke Aaron Silver's mother was Dulcina Mae Brown, a Negro, twenty-seven years of age. His father was George Martin Silver, a Caucasian, thirty-five years of age.

I looked up at him, my jaw slack.

"There it is," he declared. "Definitive proof."

"Wow," I managed. "But . . . all this time! What did you use in the past when you had to produce a birth certificate, like for school?"

Luke sat across from me. "I told you about all these Damon Runyon characters my dad was friends with," he said wearily. "I think one of them might have been a professional forger. The birth certificate I saw was completely different from this one. My 'mother' was Gina La Russo, Caucasian, age twenty-five."

I reached out and took his hand. "Your dad covered all the bases."

"That was his way," Luke said. He turned and grabbed the pizza box off the counter. "Let's have dinner, huh? I hope you don't mind if I didn't splurge . . ."

"I have something for you, too. It's a housewarming present." I handed him a bag I'd brought along with my purse. Inside was the record collection Dulcie had given me. "Consider it from me and your mom. These were her favorite singers."

He took the records without a word and placed them next to his record player. Then he walked over and kissed me. I'm not sure how much time passed, but eventually his stomach rumbled. "I think that's an impolite way of saying it's dinnertime," he murmured.

We both giggled, and he pulled away. As we ate, he flipped on the television set so we could catch the news with Walter Cronkite. The big story was something they were calling "the Great Train Robbery" in Britain. Apparently, a group of bandits made off with a pile of mailbags stuffed with more than two million pounds in banknotes.

"And you think our relatives are bad," I cracked. "How much did those guys steal in dollars, do you think?"

"About four million," Luke answered. He sighed. "At

least they have an exact number. With my dad, it's all guesswork. But I wouldn't be surprised if they turned out to be petty crooks compared to him."

When the program cut to a commercial, he turned the knob and flipped to the next channel. There was a flash of static, and we both froze. A grave anchorman, a little younger than Walter Cronkite, was talking with a picture of Lincoln Brown displayed behind him.

We held our breath as he spoke.

". . . esteemed academic, one of only two Negro professors at NYU, and the brother of the late singer Sweet Dulcie Brown. He was rushed to NYU Medical Center after an apparent suicide attempt. According to the police, he was found by a colleague who became concerned when Professor Brown did not show up for a meeting. Professor Brown survived and is expected to recover completely. Sadly, our next story . . ."

Luke turned down the sound and gaped at me. I shook my head.

"What the hell is going on?" he wondered aloud. "Was he punishing himself for killing Dulcie before someone else did?"

"Maybe Bernie is off the hook," I said. I hoped so, even though a part of me wished Lincoln Brown was innocent, too.

"First thing tomorrow, I'm going to that hospital to find out," Luke said. He put down his pizza and reached for my hand. "You with me, Watson?"

"You don't even need to ask, Mr. Holmes," I responded, squeezing back.

. . .

aNOTHEr NIGHT HOME aT the stroke of eleven, another endless day at work avoiding Bobby and Rona. I thought six o'clock would never arrive. When it did, Luke and I went straight to the hospital from the Brill Building. When we told the freckled redheaded nurse in charge that we wanted to see Professor Brown, she dashed all of the anticipation that had built over the past twenty-four hours with four words.

"Only family is allowed."

"I'm his nephew," Luke told her.

I studied her as she processed this response, watched the narrowing of the eyes that said, *You don't look like a Negro*. But Luke had foreseen this possibility. He pulled out his birth certificate, the real one. She took a look, then picked up the phone.

"Mr. Brown," she said, "your nephew is here to see you. May I send him in?"

There was a moment as she listened. Then she turned to us.

"He says he doesn't have a nephew."

"May I speak to him?" Luke deftly plucked the phone from her hands before she could protest. "I *am* your nephew, Mr. Brown," he said into the mouthpiece. "We've actually spoken before, and I have proof with me that I'm Dulcie's son."

He handed the phone back to the nurse. She listened for a moment, nodded, and hung up. "Room fifty-nine," she announced, and went back to guarding the floor.

I knew I shouldn't have been surprised, but I still was

taken aback at how vulnerable Professor Brown looked when we entered his room. Of course, lying in a hospital bed in pajamas while hooked up to IV tubes could do that to a person. He squinted at us, his shadow-rimmed eyes flashing between us as if trying to remember where he'd seen us before.

"We interviewed you for our high school, sort of," I told him.

"Tell me about the *sort of* part," he said with a weak smile.

"I'm your nephew," Luke said softly. "My dad never told me the truth about who my mother was, but I discovered it in Dulcie's memoir, and then I found my real birth certificate."

He stepped forward and handed it to Professor Brown, who scanned it and then gave it back to him with a dismissive sniff. "My crazy little sister had an affair with her manager. I'm not really surprised. Dulcie had a unique way of complicating her life."

"It wasn't just an affair, Dr. Brown; they loved each other," Luke said. "I think they would have gotten married if they could have."

Professor Brown returned Luke's stare. "Why didn't you tell me who you were when you first came to see me for the interview?"

"I wasn't ready. The only proof I had was in my mother's memoir. I wasn't about to reveal that to anyone."

Professor Brown took in the information. His tired eyes remained focused on Luke. "So how does it feel becoming a Negro at your age?" His voice hardened. "You know even if you're half white, even if you look white, even if you think of yourself as white, the world will always see you as a colored man. You know that, don't you? Once they know about your mother, you're a colored man."

"I know, and I'm trying to make that a part of me," Luke answered in an even tone. He edged closer to me. "My friend JJ here knew your sister and worked with her recently. Dulcie sang on a demonstration record of a song that we wrote together. JJ was going to have dinner with her the night she died."

Professor Brown shifted his gaze toward me. "So if you weren't writing a story for your school paper, what can you tell me about my sister that I don't know?"

"I don't believe she killed herself," I said softly. "I believe someone pushed or threw her out that window. Please excuse me for asking this question, Professor, but can you tell us where you were on the night your sister died?"

"Delivering a lecture to four hundred students," Professor Brown stated irritably, pulling himself up to a sitting position. "But I need you to tell me something. I need to know what Dulcie said about me in her memoir." He turned to Luke. "And I want to know if you intend to submit it to a publisher."

Luke seemed baffled. "We've never even thought about that. It's incomplete, and we have no way of knowing what Dulcie would have wanted, so I don't believe that we'll submit it for publication. At least that's the way I feel now. She didn't disclose anything about you, Professor Brown. She just talked about how wonderful you were as a big brother."

Professor Brown closed his eyes for a moment. "You

know, the lecture I gave that night was on ethics." He drew in a breath. "You will understand the irony of that when I tell you something I've been hiding for a very long time. To tell you the truth, I was afraid Dulcie might have revealed it in her book. I was so filled with shame. That's why . . . this happened. I thought I couldn't face the world another day."

I took a step toward his bed. "Dulcie did write that you had done something wrong. But she believed that it was up to you to reveal it or keep it hidden forever. She loved you too much to ever hurt you."

Professor Brown blinked several times and reached for a Kleenex. "I was the one who hurt myself and her. My senior year, I was the star quarterback, role model, hero. But I got involved with a girl. I neglected my schoolwork after I'd been awarded an athletic scholarship. All I had to do was pass my senior classes to keep it, but I was failing chemistry. I needed an A on the final to pass and hold on to my future. So my best friend and I hid in school until after it was closed. We jimmied the lock on the chem teacher's desk and made a copy of the test. I got to keep my scholarship. He got to graduate. It was just one class, just one transgression, but it stayed with me. It was wrong, and I knew it when I did it. It went against everything I believed in. It made me feel that I never deserved what I accomplished."

He paused and dabbed his eyes again, then took a sip of water. My pulse quickened. I was sure that the story was about to take a much darker turn—that he'd gotten his girlfriend pregnant or hurt his friend in some way to keep him quiet about what they'd done.

"Throughout my college career and beyond I knew I was a fraud and a cheat," he continued. "Dulcie found out when my best friend boasted about it to her. That's when she lost respect for me. He went to an early grave, so I knew that my secret was safe with him . . . but Dulcie carried it with her ever since. I didn't blame her. I'd been her idol, and I let her down. I've hated myself since that day. Finally I decided I just wanted peace, so . . ." He lifted his shoulders. "But I'm still here."

"I'm glad you are," Luke said.

"So am I," I added. "You saved Dulcie's life when she was a child. You gave her the love and support she wouldn't have survived without."

He cleared his throat. "That was my best time," he managed, his voice shaking. "I've done a lot of soul-searching since Dulcie's death. I've decided I'm going back home. I'm going to try and teach at our high school. Make up for what I've done by giving back."

Luke nodded, his green eyes soft. "If that's your decision, I really admire it. May I come and visit you?" he asked. He drew close to the bed.

"Of course you can," Professor Brown breathed. "You're blood, my man." He reached out and clasped Luke's hand.

Without saying a word, I stepped back into the hallway to give them a moment alone. My brain was spinning. Cheating on a test? Yes, that was a bad thing to do, but it wasn't murder. It wasn't ripping off Dulcie for the money she'd rightly earned either. He'd been a kid. Kids do dumb things all the time. My brother and I were living proof of that.

"Why are you smiling?" Luke asked as he joined me a minute later.

"Because he couldn't have killed her, for one thing," I whispered as we hurried toward the elevator. "He was giving a lecture that night. Besides, it sounds like this was a grudge that Dulcie could have let go."

"I know where you're coming from," Luke answered. He pressed the DOWN button. "I feel that way, too. But look at it from Dulcie's perspective. He was her role model. Then he betrayed that trust. Even worse, he built an entire life and image around integrity, proving that he was a different kind of Negro . . . that he was a Negro who was above reproach. But the truth is, he was a liar like every other man she knew." He looked out the window at the busy New York street below. "For her, that made him the worst kind of man. I get it."

I looped my arm in his as the elevator doors opened. I knew that Luke was beginning to see himself as Dulcie's blood, as a Negro and a man himself. I wondered if it would affect the way he felt about me. I wondered if the world would ever change in the way it looked at mixed-race couples. My parents had friends who moved to Canada to escape the prejudice they faced here in the so-called cosmopolitan city of New York. They were never accepted. Could we be?

"I won't lose you after we get to the bottom of this, will I, Luke?" I asked as the doors closed behind us and we were alone. "When the world knows who you are will you still be here with me?"

Instead of answering, he turned and kissed me on the lips.

CHAPTER THIRTY-TWO

The days that followed were the beginning of change. James Meredith became the first Negro to graduate from the University of Mississippi. The NAACP youth council began sit-ins at lunch counters in Oklahoma City. And in New York City, Detective Frank McGrath arrested Bernie Rubin for the murder of Dulcie Brown.

Uncle Bernie's arrest was all but inevitable after Marla turned in the broken necklace. Even though the evidence was circumstantial—as Luke rightly pointed out—Janny said they would continue to fish around until they scared him enough so that he would say something incriminating. He was booked at 8 A.M. on a Tuesday, so Janny allowed me to accompany her when she headed downtown to bail him out. I called Rona to tell her that I might be a little late for work owing to a family emergency. At least I wasn't lying.

On the way down, I told Janny everything I knew again, including what the Puerto Rican woman had heard before Dulcie went out the window. Apparently there was a chance

I'd have to come forth with that information, but I didn't have to do it yet. Our main objective was to get Bernie out of McGrath's clutches. Janny had already spoken to the district attorney, who told her that he intended to present Bernie's case to a grand jury for a formal indictment. And he'd definitely be indicted. For as long as I can remember, I had heard from my mom that in the criminal justice system you could indict a ham sandwich. I figured it was probably true for pastrami as well. Bernie was more the pastrami type.

Thanks to Janny's connections and Bernie's cash, he was released on bail. Then we headed back to our apartment. Juana brought out coffee and danishes, which she always did in a crisis. Bernie made it very clear that he didn't want to go back to his place. He didn't want Marla to be a part of the conversation. He filled us in on the fact that she'd actually told him about finding the necklace, just as I had asked her to. The trouble was, she had told him after she had gone to McGrath. She hadn't given him a chance to defend himself as she'd promised me. Then he'd flipped out. The two of them had a real screamer. He hadn't seen her since. And now . . .

"Bernie," Janny said, cutting him off, "where were you the night Dulcie died? If you have an alibi, this is all moot."

"I don't have an alibi," Bernie admitted. "I was working. Even though it was a Saturday, I had things to catch up on."

"When you left, did you take the elevator?" I asked. "Maybe Nick saw you."

"No, I took the stairs because there was only one elevator

working that late. I think it was Antonio's. Whatever. I was in a hurry to get home."

Janny set her coffee cup down. "Did you speak to anyone on the phone between six and seven?" she asked.

"I know I'm not making this easy for you, Janice, but the answer is no." Bernie hadn't touched his own coffee or danish. "The bottom line is I could have done it, but I didn't. You're just going to have to believe me."

"What I believe is irrelevant," Janny shot back. "It's what I can prove. The problem lies with your reputation. You've been involved with gangsters, with payola, with a thousand rotten music business schemes—all of which, I might add, have not gone unnoticed by the police. This is *Les Miz* in the Brill Building. McGrath is your Inspector Javert. You're his Jean Valjean. He wants you in prison for something. He's been keeping an eye on you. And he's frustrated that he hasn't been able to nail you yet. But when and if he does, he knows that the impression you will give to a jury is not going to be a good one."

Bernie glanced at me. For a second, I almost thought I caught a glimpse of that old twinkle, that bravado I'd come to both loathe and love. "You don't like me very much, do you, sis?" he asked, his tone dry. "I mean, I just want to determine if that's 'relevant' or not."

"I can never forgive the pain you caused our parents by dropping out of their lives," she stated.

"Spoken like a true lawyer—neither a yes nor a no." Bernie shook his head. "I'm not the most solid citizen, there's no denying it," he continued, "but I want you to know something, Janice. I had a pretty good reason for not coming around. Our parents called my first wife, whom I adored, 'the spic' behind her back. Margarita knew how they felt about her. That she was unworthy of being included in our family. That's not why we split, but it sure didn't help our marriage. And Janice, you took their side. You shut me out completely. Why do you think I showed up at Jeff's bar mitzvah? I wanted you to see how much our family meant to me. I wanted back in, but you never opened the door."

I turned to my mother. From the shock on her face, I could see that this side of her parents was just as much of a revelation to her as it was to me.

"I hear what you're saying, Bernie," Janny said. "I do." Her voice was tight. She smoothed her skirt. "Putting our past aside, I'm only going to ask you this one time. So think carefully before you answer me. Did you kill Dulcie Brown?"

"No," Bernie replied without hesitation. "I did not. Now I'm only going to ask you this one time, and I want the truth, too. Do you believe me?"

I watched them stare at each other, trying not to let their years of history get in the way of this moment. Janny opened her mouth, then closed it. She was pleading the fifth. A true lawyer, indeed.

"Okay, Jan," Bernie muttered, leaning back. "I get it. Can you represent me anyway?"

"Of course I can." Janny said, with a sad smile. "I do it all the time."

Later That Morning at Good Music, I copied and filed as usual. Rona left me alone, knowing I was coping with unspecified family drama. Maybe that would shield me from Bobby, too. On every break, I played Dulcie's demo of "I'm Glad I Did" over and over. Maybe if I just listened closely enough, I might find some answers. A message of some kind in the turn of a phrase, the lyricism of a vocal riff or just the sound of her voice. I knew it didn't make sense, but she was right there in the room with me.

"Tell me," I whispered. "Tell me what happened."

My mother thought Bernie was guilty. I was still trying to wrap my head around that, but then as I listened to the demo, I had a thought. It had nothing to do with Dulcie's death, but her voice led me to it. *I know who might be able to record Dulcie's demo. I know a singer who isn't on the usual Good Music list, a singer Bobby Goodman can discover . . .*

First I called Luke to run the idea by him. Then I called Rosetta, who was her usual warm and fuzzy self. "What do *you* want, girl?" she grunted. I asked her to pick up the demo at the Good Music office, just to give it a listen, to see how her mother had brought life to a song. She was guarded until I told her that there would be no hugging involved. Then I decided to take a lunch break at The Turf bar.

I'd been chomping on my sandwich for about five minutes when Nick slid onto the seat next to me. I don't think I'd ever been as happy to see him. I needed company, an ear. I felt as if my thoughts were driving holes in my brain. I needed to hear someone else's voice.

"Please talk to me," I said. "I'm obsessing about Dulcie again. I'm driving myself crazy."

"I've been thinking about her, too," Nick confessed.

"She'd been through so much, and she was still such a sweet person. She was so alive . . . it's hard to believe that she's gone. It breaks my heart."

He ordered roast beef on a bun and a Coke.

"It breaks my heart, too," I answered. "What's worse is that I really believed she had a good chance for a comeback."

"I know," Nick confirmed. "She sounded fantastic on that song of yours she recorded."

"Yeah, she did," I said. "I mean, that's what gave me the idea . . ." All at once, I felt a stab in my gut. I wasn't sure why, but I knew I had to get off the subject of Dulcie. "I don't think I can talk about it anymore," I told Nick. "You know everything that's going on in the building. Fill me in on some juicy gossip."

He was happy to oblige. In the next five minutes, I found out who was delivering payola money to which disc jockey, who was cheating on their wives—and the only gossip that truly interested me—who was getting their songs recorded and by whom. But all the time he was talking, I felt a silent alarm going off in my brain. Something was wrong.

Right after lunch, I sneaked down from Good Music to room 717. Luke had almost finished packing. Gone were the stacks of papers and piles of folders; almost everything was in boxes now. He was starting to take the pictures off the walls . . . and then he'd be done.

"Luke, did you ever play Dulcie's demo for Nick?" I asked, not bothering to sit.

"No." He shook his head. "I never played it for anyone. Why do you ask?"

That's when it hit me. In that instant I knew what I did and didn't want to know. If Luke hadn't played it for Nick, and I hadn't played it for Nick, there was only one other place he could have heard it: Dulcie's apartment. But he had told me that he'd never been there.

"Why would he do that?" I asked Luke, once I'd spelled everything out for him. "Why would he lie?"

"Maybe he just misspoke," Luke countered. His green eyes got that distant look they always did when he was thinking deeply about something, weighing all the various outcomes. "Maybe he didn't want you to know he'd been there for his own reasons. There are so many maybes."

"Yeah, there are." I met his gaze. "But maybe the only one that matters is he lied."

"JJ," Luke said in a soft voice, "are you sure you're not jumping on this because you don't want Bernie to be guilty?"

"I'm sure," I answered. "Luke . . . I can't explain it. I have this feeling inside. Like I'm connected to Dulcie, and she's telling me what to do. I'm going to McGrath, and I'm going to tell him what I know and what I think."

Luke stepped toward me, taking my hands. "I'm sure the New York City police department will be eager to discuss the vibrations you feel from beyond the grave," he commented dryly, raising his eyebrows.

I had to smile even though I didn't want to. At least he smiled back. That smile was worth any grief. "You're probably right, Sherlock, but I'm going to tell them anyway."

He let go of my hands and kissed me on the lips. "I

know you will, Watson. Just call me when you do. I'll be wrapping up here. I can't wait to hear how they respond to your theory. My advice: just go easy on the Dulcie communication part."

CHAPTER THIRTY-THREE

fter work I took the stairs down from Good Music
instead of the elevator, then hopped on the subway
to police headquarters—all the way downtown. By
the time I arrived forty minutes later, I was hot and tired.
And surprised at how crummy the place was, on par with
Luke's apartment. The main floor was grimy and chaotic:
sweaty cops bringing in sweatier criminals and booking
them. People shuffled in, milling around, looking for
jailed relatives. And there were some real nutcases: some
yelling about their innocence, some screaming they
didn't belong there, others screaming for no reason at all.
I couldn't conceive of the kind of person who'd actually
want to work here.

Luckily, the wait was short. I was ushered into Frank
McGrath's office after only a few minutes. I didn't even let
him get through the usual pleasantries before I launched
into the story of my lunch with Nick, and the slip he'd
made in regard to Dulcie and visiting her apartment.

"Only three people had the demo," I finished. "Luke, me, and Dulcie, and neither Luke nor I played it for him. The only place he could have heard it was Dulcie's apartment on the afternoon or night of her death. You need to at least question him."

He leaned back in his chair and motioned toward one across from the desk. "Justice, you sure you don't want to sit?"

"No, thank you."

"Listen, sweetheart," McGrath said with poorly disguised sarcasm, "I'm sure your mom has told you we're understaffed and need help. So I really appreciate your trying to assist us in this investigation. But right now we have a suspect who is very viable. We're very busy and focused on checking into his involvement in this case."

"You're talking about my Uncle Bernie, aren't you?"

"Yes, at this moment, Bernie Rubin is our prime suspect. But we will definitely look into this Nick person, the elevator operator." He sat up and straightened a pile of papers, then reached for a notebook.

I knew I was being "yessed." I could tell by the tone of his voice and the look in his eyes. *Shut the little girl up, and get her out of here so she won't bother us anymore.*

"Please, Detective McGrath," I begged. "Please take this as seriously as if a person over twenty-one was telling you this. My uncle may not be guilty."

McGrath stifled a grin. But he clicked open a pen and leaned over his notebook. "Okay, JJ. I'll run a make on your suspect. Now, what's Nick's last name?"

I felt my heart stop. I didn't know Nick's last name. He

was just Nick. "Um, I . . . I, I'll find that out for you and call you," I stammered.

"You do that," McGrath said, letting the grin escape. His lips curved into a gentle smile. "And then you get back to me."

I think I managed to escape his office without tripping over my big feet because they were planted firmly in my mouth. What kind of Watson was I? And what kind of advocate for Bernie? My face felt hot, and I knew I was probably bright red. I didn't know what to do. I just knew I had to tell Janny what I'd learned and what I'd done before I screwed up anymore.

I found a pay phone and called her office. She was still in court. I left word with her secretary that I had something important to discuss with Janny, along with Luke's office number. Then, I called Luke and told him exactly how I'd made a total fool of myself. At least I hadn't mentioned trying to communicate with Dulcie through her vocal performance.

"Do you know Nick's last name?" I asked.

"What kind of question is that, Watson?"

"Well, Sherlock, it seems they need that to run a make on him, and I don't know it."

"Well, er . . . why don't you come over to the office?"

I had to laugh. "You don't either. Are we lame or what, Sherlock? Can you guess?"

"I never guess," Luke stated with a fairly spot-on Holmes-like British accent. "It is a shocking habit—destructive to the logical faculty."

"I get it, wise guy. You know your Sherlock quotes, but you don't know Nick's last name. I'm on my way."

. . .

aNOTHer FOrTY MINUTes OF being jammed in a stuffy subway car, and I was back at the Brill Building, none the wiser or happier. It was almost eight o'clock. I was exhausted. The last bit of sunlight was fading from the city streets. I marched through the lobby, planning to take the stairs to Luke's office—but all at once, Nick's elevator door opened.

"Hey, kiddo," he called. "Your chariot awaits."

What was I going to say? That I'd rather climb seven flights of stairs than ride in an elevator with him? I managed a smile and nodded.

"Going to Luke's," I said casually, stepping inside.

"Your personal express, kiddo." Nick smiled. "I think you two might have the building to yourself."

I knew I should be making conversation as I always did, but the words caught in my throat. My pulse began to race. The elevator had never felt so small or confining, not even in the mornings when we were all jammed together like cattle. I swallowed, staring at the dial. Only two more floors to go . . .

The car suddenly lurched. He'd stopped. Between the sixth and seventh floors.

"Whoops," I said. "What's wrong?"

Nick leaned against the elevator wall and stared at me intently. "I made a mistake, didn't I?" It was a rhetorical question.

"What do you mean?" I asked. I tried to sound cheery and unaware, even though I was sure he could hear my heart thumping.

"I saw it in your eyes, kiddo. When I told you I heard the demo. She told me she had the only copy besides yours, so you knew I was there the night she died."

I felt myself backing up against the opposite wall, but there was nowhere to go. I had to see this conversation through to its end, whatever that would mean. Best just to take charge, to put him at ease. He knew he was doomed; there was nothing he could do now.

"Yes, I knew," I said.

"I didn't kill her," Nick told me in a choked voice. "Please believe me. I went to see her because I couldn't hold my feelings in any longer. I did so much for her. I kept everything that went on between her and your uncle a secret, even though it tore me up. I even covered for Bernie when the cops came sniffing around." He snorted in disgust. "He's a dog, kiddo, when it comes to the ladies. He doesn't care about anyone but himself. But I'm different. I really cared about Dulcie, and I thought maybe she'd come to care for me, too." His eyes were pleading with me. His voice sounded desperate.

"So what happened?" I asked, my heart pounding.

"I can't tell you," he said.

"Listen, Nick, my mom's a lawyer." My speech sounded fast and high-pitched in my ears, but I plowed forward. "She'll help you, I promise. You'll be okay, but you have to tell the truth. Can you just take me to seven now?"

Nick didn't seem to hear me. "They think Bernie did it. It's all over the building. He'll never get convicted of something he didn't do. He's too smart for that." His eyes locked with mine. "It'll all be fine, but I can't have you telling anybody anything. You've got to give me your word that you won't. Make me believe you, kiddo, please."

I knew that if I promised him, my face would give me away. There was no way I wasn't going to the police. He would know. This was bad. I could feel panic rising in both of us. I knew I had to get out of that elevator box. I didn't know what he would do, but I did know he was cornered—and when someone is cornered, they don't necessarily behave true to form.

Maybe that explained what happened next. Because something inside me snapped.

I've been a klutz my whole life, except for my fingers. I was always the last one chosen for every team I ever wanted to be on. But when Nick stepped toward me, I sidestepped him and lunged for the crank that operated the elevator. He tried to pull me away, but I stomped on his instep with my heel—a trick Janny had taught me as soon as I was old enough to wear heels—and managed to stop the car approximately on the seventh floor. I tried to pull the door open, but Nick grabbed my arm.

"Stop it, JJ," he hissed. "I need to talk to you."

I did the only thing I could think of to make him let go. I bit his hand. It was a horrible, weird feeling to clamp down on human flesh. But the moment he cried out and released my arm, I pulled the door open. I was nowhere near level with the seventh floor, maybe two feet too high, but I jumped down and fell like the lummox I truly was.

The next thing I knew, I found myself breathing heavily into Nick's face, our noses only inches apart.

The last time I had been in this position, Jeff's face had

been the one hovering over mine—another wrestling victory of his, while my parents stood by, not interfering on principle. Jeff's expression had been one of smug satisfaction. Nick's was one of panic. He'd pinned my arms. I could smell his lunch and coffee on his breath. "Please, JJ," he croaked. "You're gonna get me in trouble."

I guess it was a good thing that our parents never interfered in our fights. Who would have ever guessed it, but the course in Brazilian judo finally paid off—six years after the fact. The one move I'd mastered, the upward lift escape, came back to me. It shot from the recesses of my memory straight into my arms and legs. With a loud grunt, I sent Nick flying off me. I scrambled to my feet and stumbled across the hall, diving into Luke's office a second before Nick came careening through the door after me.

Luke was almost six feet tall, in perfect condition, while Nick was barely five six. His only exercise in years had been pulling open an elevator door. It was no contest. Luke grabbed him, pinned his arms to his side, pushed him into a chair and held him there.

"Tell me what's going on," Luke commanded. He wasn't even breathing heavily. In truth, he was terrifying. And I'd never been more relieved to be terrified in my life as I cowered behind him. His voice had so much authority that Nick stopped struggling. "Now!"

Nick nodded and blurted out what he had told me. And then he crumbled. He actually dissolved into tears, crying for Dulcie, for what had happened to her and for himself.

Steeling my nerves, I climbed out from behind Luke

and kneeled in front of Nick. "Look, you have to come clean," I said. "Tell us what happened that night."

He wiped his eyes with the sleeve of his uniform. "I've played it over in my head so many times. It's like a movie I can't stop watching."

"Play it for us now, Nick," Luke encouraged him, his voice gentle now. "We can't help you until we know what went down. And I promise we will help."

Nick mustered what little self-possession he had left. "It took me all day to get up the courage to go to her apartment," he explained. "But I had to find out what she was feeling toward me. She was so kind and so beautiful. When I got there, she was cleaning broken dishes off the floor and playing the demo. She was really upset. So I took my time and helped her reset the table, and then I told her. I told her how I felt about her, that I loved her and I knew she had never been treated the way she deserved to be. That I would be kind to her and never take advantage of her." He sniffed. "And her words . . . I'll never forget. 'Just what I need,' she said, 'another white man to take care of me.'"

I shook my head. The connection I'd felt, that belief that Dulcie was right there with me, had never felt stronger. Nick was indeed the projector, rolling the film for us.

"But I wasn't just another *anything*," Nick went on. "I was someone who loved her. She told me I'd better go. She was expecting someone for dinner. I guess I raised my voice. I told her how much I loved her. And then she shouted something back at me. Something almost exactly like what my mother said when she left. Like . . . word for word. 'I can't help how I feel. Don't try and make me feel guilty.'"

I winced at his pain. Luke did, too. It was impossible not to feel for him. He was so lonely, so lost. He'd suffered more than anybody should suffer.

Nick's were eyes glassy now, staring at nothing. "I guess I went a little nuts. I grabbed her. I wanted to shake some sense into her. I was wrong, I know I was wrong, and then she pulled away and backed up. The window was wide open, 'cause it was so hot that night. When she turned, she slid on a record sleeve that was on the floor. She lost her footing, tripped, and the next thing I knew, she was out the window. It was a nightmare. I just ran to escape it . . ." He bowed his head, finished.

Luke's hand touched my shoulder. I clasped it, drawing strength from it, and let it go. "Nick, my mom is the best criminal attorney in New York," I told him. "She's been through this hundreds of times. She won't let anything bad happen to you. I promise."

Nick looked up. "I don't know if I care what happens to me now. It almost feels good to have it all out," he whispered. "I don't want to go to prison, but I hate myself so much, I don't want to be free either."

"Don't say that," Luke said. "Please don't say you hate yourself. I see the pain you're in. And I forgive you. Please listen to this with your heart as well as your head. After she died, I learned that Dulcie was my mother. If I can find a way to grieve for her *and* for you, then you can do it, too."

Nick closed his eyes. "My God, Luke? Your mother . . . I . . . I'm so, so sorry . . . I . . . ." He began to weep.

Now Luke put his arms around Nick, not to restrain him but to console him.

In that moment I knew that my feelings for Luke were more than I'd given them credit for. I hadn't just fallen for a crush. This wasn't just my first summer fling. He was a boy I could really love. The *man* I could love, no matter what the future had in store. His words had been spot-on, but not about me, about him. *Something like a miracle.*

CHapTer THirTY-Four

Once we called Janny and Nick turned himself into the police, things got a lot more complicated very quickly, much more than I'd hoped or imagined. It turned out that Janny just couldn't step in and represent Nick. Also, Luke and I had to be far more involved than I'd assumed. Janny always did everything by the book, and the legal maneuvering was tricky, even though the truth was clear. First, Luke and I had to tell McGrath, on the record and with Janny present, what we knew about Nick's involvement with Dulcie's death. Only then, once Bernie was cleared by the information we gave the police—and both Bernie and Nick had waived confidentiality—could she step in and represent Nick.

By now Nick was so broken by finally admitting his part in Dulcie's death that he would have done anything Janny had asked him. She explained that there was a good chance he might be convicted of a misdemeanor because he'd left the scene, that he might have to spend some time in custody. But Janny assured him that ultimately she was confident she could clear him for murder. It was an accident. He was grateful but responded that he didn't even deserve her help. He deserved whatever time in custody that he got. Janny told him they would talk about that once he had a chance to pull himself together.

Even though Luke wanted to stay by my side, I told him to go home. It was late, and he'd done more than enough to help. With Janny's prying eyes on us, he couldn't kiss me goodbye, though he did manage to squeeze my hand. I told him I'd talk to him tomorrow at work. Luckily, Janny didn't ask me any questions. After that she called Bernie from the police station. It was almost ten o'clock at night, but he was still at his office.

He didn't sound particularly overjoyed at being exonerated. He told Janny cryptically that he had been "doing some thinking." He instructed us to meet in front of his apartment. Janny reminded him of the late hour, but he insisted that we both come, and that he wanted me there, too. Then he asked to speak to me. Janny handed me the phone.

"I want you both with me for this," he said.

"For what?" I asked. "What is 'this'?"

"Please just be there. I need you both. Okay, Justice, baby?"

"Okay, Uncle Bernie. I'll be there."

I handed the phone back to my mom, who hung up. The second our eyes met, we nodded. I had a feeling something bad was going to happen, but still I wasn't scared. For once in our lives, Janny and I were connected, on the same team, fighting the same fight. It was a moment to be savored.

Bernie gave us each a quick hug when we met him in his apartment building lobby. That same drawn, sallow look I'd seen at The Turf was back. Without a word, he walked us to the elevator. I couldn't read what he was feeling, but I knew Bernie. When he became unemotional, it was because he was enraged. Now I could tell by the set of his jaw that he was seething about something.

"Don't ask me anything," he warned us as we rode up to his apartment.

As we entered, we could hear Marla puttering around in the kitchen. When the door closed behind us, there was a cry of delight. "Bernard!" she shrieked.

I couldn't help but feel a little cynical, older than my years. So she'd forgiven him just like that. Even though he'd lied to her and cheated on her. She'd forgiven him because she wasn't going to lose anything. I wondered how much she really loved Bernie the man or how much she loved living this fabulous music biz life in this flashy apartment.

"Come in here, baby. We've got some company," he said.

Marla bounded into the foyer, threw her arms around Bernie and blew us kisses. "He's forgiven me for going to the police before telling him," she murmured, nuzzling his neck. "Bernie knew I had to do what I had to do."

"Yes, I forgave you for your flash of integrity." He glanced at Janny. "One person in every family should have integrity at any given time, right?" Bernie withdrew from Marla's embrace and smiled, but his eyes were cold. "Sit down now, Marla. I want to talk to you."

Marla's forehead creased as she sat in an armchair. Janny and I eased onto the couch, hoping to make her more comfortable. But Bernie remained standing. "You were working pretty hard to try and frame me for Dulcie's murder," he said calmly. "As you can well imagine, I'm a little upset about it."

Janny swallowed audibly. I stiffened on the couch.

"What are you talking about, Bernard?" Marla's voice quavered.

"I'm usually a stickler for details, so I'm a little ashamed to admit that it took me a few days to figure this out. But there was only one possible way that necklace could have gotten into my pocket. You put it there. And there was only one possible reason for you to do that: so that I would be convicted of Dulcie Brown's murder. So now why don't you tell me how *you* got the necklace? Don't bother inventing anything. There's no point."

Marla squirmed in her seat. A flow of emotions played across her face, and finally, maybe because there was no other recourse, she was the one who got down on her knees in front of Bernie. I almost rolled my eyes. The two of them were as dramatic as Richard Burton and Elizabeth Taylor.

"Please forgive me, darling," she babbled. "I should have told you, but I was so ashamed. I went through your phone bill. There was one number that kept popping up, so I had it traced. Bernard, when I saw that it belonged to Dulcie Brown, I thought I would die on the spot. I was so

jealous, I couldn't contain myself. I went to see her, to beg her to break it off with you. She told me that she was sorry, but you and she had a bond and a history. She said that that you were going to leave me for her. I saw that necklace she wore, and I just knew it had been a gift from you. The table was set for dinner, and you had told me you were working late at the office, so I had a feeling that it was for you, Bernard—"

"It wasn't for Bernie," I interrupted. Everyone turned. "It was for me. I was supposed to have dinner with Dulcie that night."

"My God," Marla breathed. "It's what put me over the edge. I pulled at the tablecloth so all the dishes would break. She came at me, and I ripped that damn necklace off her and ran." She turned back to Bernie, clasping her hands in front of her. "I believed her. I believed that you— my husband, who I loved more than life—would leave me. I couldn't bear that. I wanted to hurt you, Bernard, the way you had hurt me . . ." She began to sob quietly at Bernie's feet.

He looked down at her as if she was some alien life form he'd never seen before. His eyes were curious, but his gaze cut through her hysteria like a knife. He pulled her gently to her feet, lifted her chin and looked into her tearful eyes. "I'm going to a hotel for three days," he said. "I expect you to be gone when I get back. My lawyer—not my sister, my attorney who's a lot less forgiving and has a heart of stone—will get in touch with you. From him, you'll find out what you'll need to do to. As for me, I only want one thing. That's never to see you again."

With that he turned and beckoned for us to follow him. Marla crumpled to the floor, sobbing.

He paused for a moment at the door. "You know, Marla, George gave me seven to three that we wouldn't last five years. It's the only bet I ever took that I knew I'd lose."

CHAPTER THIRTY-FIVE

ernie could be cold-hearted and tough, yes—and even crooked—but he did have a heart. He actually put up the money for Nick's bail. Janny engineered Nick's release based on the fact that he had never even gotten so much as a parking ticket. He had a regular job, a spotless record as an employee, and was a respected member of the community. He'd decided to take a few days off until everything was sorted out and while Janny worked on a plea. Since he hadn't taken a sick day in thirteen years, no one objected.

The next day in the elevator, with Antonio at the helm, there was a lot of speculation about where Nick was, since the news hadn't hit the papers yet, but no one had a clue as to the real reason. And amazingly, like everyone else, I missed him. But now I had to put that aside. Now I had real work to do.

AFTER CHECKING THE ARTISTS' list on the bulletin board, I waited for Rona to take a break and put in a call to Luke. "Listen," I said, "Ray Charles is on the list today. Bobby wants to pitch a song to him, and Dulcie was like a female Ray Charles."

"So you want to play him her demo of 'I'm Glad I Did'?"

"Sort of. I want to play him that song but not Dulcie's demo. Can you meet me at Dick Charles at six sharp?"

I could hear that smile through the phone. "What are we up to?"

"You'll see," I promised. I hung up just as Rona returned. "Would you set up an appointment for me with Bobby tomorrow?"

Her face lit up. "You playing him something?"

"Abso-elvis-lutely," I said.

She grinned. "Atta girl. It's about time."

Rosetta showed up at the studio at six on the dot. "I gotta be at work at seven," she reminded us.

"Do you know the song?" Luke asked.

"What kind of question is that?" she barked. No doubt about it, Rosetta was Anna Mae Brown's granddaughter. Everything was a challenge, and nobody was any good.

"He just wanted to know if you needed to rehearse while Brooks was setting up the microphone," I explained as gently as I could.

"Am I getting paid for this?" she demanded.

"How's twenty bucks?" Luke proposed.

She shrugged. "Better than nothing." With that, she headed into the studio, slipped on the headphones and glared at the three of us through the control room glass.

Brooks got some levels and then looked up at me. I pressed the TALK BACK button. "You ready for a take?"

Rosetta nodded. Brooks cued the musical track from Dulcie's session. My plan was to replace Dulcie's vocal with her daughter's. Luke loved the idea. And fortunately Rosetta had the same range as her mother, so singing in the same key was perfect.

When the sound of the musicians playing that song came up on the speaker, I felt a pang in my chest. It transported me instantly back to that night. When Dulcie's voice kicked in, my throat tightened. Luke reached over and squeezed my hand.

Something was happening to Rosetta, too. She was actually smiling. She shook her head and looked at us. For the first time ever, I saw doubt in those icy eyes.

"I really like this song," she said softly into the mic. "Mama sang on that demo like she meant it. I don't know if I can sing it as good as her."

"Just sing it as good as you, Rosetta," Luke told her from the control room.

Brooks rewound the tape and this time left Dulcie's vocal out. It was time for Rosetta to sing it her way. It was strange, but she seemed to become another person when she sang, softer and more sensitive. Her vocal quality had traces of Dulcie's huskiness, but what she added was all hers. It was tougher but more innocent, too—with youthful passion and a sense of hope for the future.

Twenty minutes later, we had it in three takes, just like with Dulcie. If she'd done it one more time, I would have dissolved into tears. As I watched Luke give Rosetta a thumbs-up through the window, I suddenly knew who he had written the words for.

"This was for your dad, wasn't it?" I asked, turning to him.

He nodded, his eyes still on Rosetta. "Like I said, JJ Green, you get me."

rosetta came into the control room and listened back with us. I could tell she was pleased, though she would never admit it.

Luke took out a twenty. "Thank you for sharing your talent with us," he said, his tone businesslike and professional.

Rosetta shook her head. "Keep your money," she told him. "I can't take it. I was lucky to sing that beautiful song." She turned to go.

"May I speak to you privately for a moment?" Luke asked her.

"I guess so."

He followed her into the waiting room and closed the control room door behind them.

"What's that about?" Brooks asked.

"I'm not sure," I told him. "Let's get a quick mix."

It took us about fifteen minutes. We cut some acetates, and finally Luke walked back in. Brooks took the opportunity to take a cigarette break.

"I told her who I was," Luke confided once Brooks was gone.

I swept him into my arms. "How did she react?"

"There was hugging involved." Luke pulled back and grinned. "She didn't seem to mind this time."

CHAPTER THIRTY-SIX

Our appointment with Bobby was set for three o'clock.
But I had to face facts: the summer would be over
soon. Even if Bobby liked our song, there was no way
he could go out with it, pitch it, and assure me of a record
before I started school on September ninth. I tried not to
think about the agreement I had made with Janny. Rona
had been right to nag me. I had gotten so caught up with
Luke and Dulcie's death and Bernie that I hadn't realized
that the days were slipping away. And I knew Janny well
enough to know that I couldn't fudge it: a song of mine had
to be guaranteed to be on a record before school began.

There was no way it could happen. Even the speediest
record producers hung on to a whole batch of songs for
weeks before they made their decisions. I had found a col-
laborator I wanted to work with for the rest of my life, and
I had written my best, but I was still going to lose. Even if
Bobby loved it and agreed to play it for Ray Charles, we
were too late.

"Knock 'em dead, kids," Rona whispered with an encouraging smile as she ushered us into Bobby's office.

I introduced Luke as my lyricist and told Bobby we had something to play for him that we thought would be perfect for Ray Charles. I told him not to get thrown by the fact that we had put a female vocal on it. We had chosen the singer because of her talent and not her gender.

"Never give excuses before you play something. Especially something I've been waiting months for," Bobby returned. "Just give me the demo."

The only person who could intimidate me more than Janny was the man seated in front of me. I bit my lip and handed him the record. He slipped it on the turntable, dropped the needle, sat back and closed his eyes.

As the intro to "I'm Glad I Did" began to play over Bobby's huge speakers, Luke reached for my hand. I was instinctively reaching for his. We met halfway. As we listened, I knew we had done the right thing.

> *And I'm glad I did, though it may hurt me now.*
> *I loved you as long as our time would allow.*
> *Yes, I'm glad I did, and I treasure what we had*
> *With all we went through I was blessed to love you*
> *Through the good times and the bad*
> *I'm glad . . . so glad I did.*

Whatever Bobby thought, Rosetta's performance was gold. Whatever he thought, I was proud of the song and the demo. That was something I could live with.

When it was over, he opened his eyes and muttered,

"She sounds like someone." But when I tried to tell him who, he shushed me. Then he replaced the needle at the beginning and closed his eyes again.

Luke looked at me as if to say, *Is this what he does?*

I shrugged. I had no idea. I figured he was taking mental notes on all the things he didn't like about it.

We sat through it a second time. By this time, our clasped hands were getting sweaty. The third time Bobby put it on, I had to unclasp Luke's hand to wipe the corner of my eye, where a big, fat tear was trying to escape.

When the demo ended for the third time, I was sure it the worst song I'd ever heard. I hated it.

Bobby opened his eyes. "It's not for Ray Charles," was his verdict. "I can't get past the female vocal."

I felt my heart sink into my shoes. My first big decision of my music career, and I was wrong. If there was a word that was wronger than wrong, I was that word.

"Bobby, I know you can get past the female vocal." I tried not to sound whiny or pleading, without much luck.

"I don't want to try," Bobby told us. "Good Music is limiting me. I'm starting my own record company, Good Records. We're going to be distributed by RCA."

Luke elbowed me. "So what are you saying, sir?"

"What I'm saying is, if I like what you tell me about her, I want this girl to be the first artist I sign and this song to be her first release."

My mouth fell open. "You . . . you . . . you like it that much?"

"I told you to write about love," Bobby said. "And look at you. You found a lyricist who could do it. I'm almost never wrong about these things." He cocked an eyebrow. "It's not what I usually like. It's not what the business is expecting from me. But I like that, and it gives me that hit feeling I can't explain." He smiled. "Now tell me who she is."

"Her name is Rosetta Brown," Luke told him, while I tried to recover. "She sounds like Dulcie Brown because she's her daughter."

Bobby's smile widened. "Is that a fact? How old is she?"

Luke shrugged. "Twenty-five, I think."

"So she's a little old, but we can shave a few years off, and she's got a story, coming from that family. I can work with it. Just tell me she looks like her mother."

"She does," we said in unison.

Luke laughed. "Tell him how beautiful she is, JJ."

"She's drop-dead gorgeous," I confirmed.

Bobby leaned forward and pressed his intercom button. "Rona, get me songwriter contracts for Luke—what's your last name?"

"Silver," Luke responded.

He blinked. "You George Silver's kid?"

Luke nodded and looked him squarely in the eye. "I am, and I'm Dulcie Brown's son, too. How's that for your story?"

I held my breath, waiting for Bobby's reaction.

He actually laughed out loud, then pressed the intercom button again. "Make those contracts long term for Luke and JJ. Give 'em each a guarantee of fifty bucks a week."

"Abso-elvis-lutely." I could hear Rona's whoop of joy over the intercom.

Bobby frowned at us. "Why are you two sitting there, grinning like idiots? I need three more songs for her session. Now the real work begins."

CHAPTER THIRTY-SEVEN

I came down early to breakfast the next morning. The truth was, I had been so excited about what had happened with the demo, I couldn't sleep all night. It was one of the few times in Green family history that I was the first one at the table. Juana brought me my coffee and bran muffin, smiling because she could sense I had a really good secret. I smiled back until Jeffrey showed up.

"Top of the mornin' to ya, little sister," he greeted me, plopping down in his chair.

"Good morning, Jeffrey," I mumbled.

"So, JJ, I've been meaning to talk to you about something."

Uh-oh. It was the first time he hadn't called me "Irving" in years. And since we were pretty much alone—just Juana, no Mom and Dad to act as a buffer—I wondered what annoying little plan for me was brewing under that slicked-back hair.

"I can't imagine what," I returned.

"Well, here's the thing. I met this girl—"

"So you want advice about girls," I interrupted. "Here it is. Whatever you're thinking: hold off for a while."

His lips twisted in a grin. "I don't want advice. It's just that when I was telling her about you, you know, about my family, I realized something."

"I'm afraid to ask what," I muttered.

"I haven't been very nice to you for a very long time."

I nearly dropped my muffin. This from the boy who had never once admitted he was wrong about anything. But I managed to recover quickly. "How about since birth?"

He couldn't help but smile. "Seriously, I think I know the reason now."

"Do tell," I said. "Better late than never."

"Just cut me some slack here, JJ, all right? It isn't easy to admit, so give me points for that. The reason is because you always had the guts to stand up to Mom and Dad and do what you believed in, and I didn't. The whole music thing. You never gave up on it. But I never had it in me to go against them. I toed the party line."

I stared at him, not believing my ears. "You mean, you don't want to be a lawyer?"

"JJ, I never ever allowed myself to think about being anything else, so I don't know."

He looked so vulnerable that what happened next was as much a shock to me as it was to him. I got up and put my arms around him, maybe for the first time ever. "You'll make a great lawyer," I told him. "You negotiated the hell out of our bathroom deal. It's why I had all those bladder infections when I was little."

He laughed and hugged me back. "So," he said, "I want to call a truce. I promise not to call you Irving anymore as a symbol of the new me."

"Bad idea. I think you should keep calling me Irving just so Mom and Dad don't freak out," I told him, returning to my seat.

"What was that about Mom and Dad freaking out?" asked Jules as he and Janny entered the dining room.

"I've asked a friend to join us for breakfast," I piped up, quickly covering for Jeffrey—again, maybe for the first time ever. "I hope you won't freak out."

"Is it this Rona you're always talking about?"

"No, it's my friend Luke Silver. Mom's met him. He's a lyricist . . . my lyricist. He'll be here any minute."

Jeff bit his lip, probably from making a crack at my expense—old habits die hard, after all—as Jules retired behind his paper with a "that's nice." As he opened it, I couldn't help but notice an article headlined MARCH ON WASHINGTON FOR JOBS AND FREEDOM SET FOR AUGUST 28.

"Mom," I said, "I want to thank you for everything you're doing for Nick. I know it's all pro bono, and I'm grateful."

"I'm proud that you know what *pro bono* means," Janny answered with a smile. "The trajectory measurements of the body seem to confirm Nick's story that she fell through the open window. It may take a while but I know he'll be cleared."

"And then what will happen?" I asked.

"He tells me he wants to get away from New York and

The Brill Building," Janny responded. "He wants to go back to Greece. I'm encouraging him to do that."

I breathed a sigh of relief. Then I pulled myself together to share my news.

"And now I have something to tell all of you," I announced. "Get ready. Luke and I wrote a song together, and we have our first record deal. It's being released by Bobby Goodman's new record company, and the artist is Rosetta Brown, Dulcie's daughter."

"Congrats, Irving. I'm surprised but not surprised, if you know what I mean. I had a feeling you'd pull off the impossible," the new Jeff declared, breaking the silence.

Janny tried to match my brother's smile but couldn't quite pull it off. She sighed. "I can't say I'm over the moon with joy. But I've come to see that you have a good head on your shoulders. I realize that I can't protect you from every bad thing in life, no matter what you end up doing for a living. I am very proud of you, Justice. I'll respect our deal."

"I will as well," Jules said in his serious judge voice. "And I must say I admire what you did for your friend Dulcie."

"So do I," Janny added. "You stood your ground."

"Thanks." I met my mother's gaze. "Mom, you know no matter how much I look up to you, I can't be another you. I can only be the best me I can be, and I've stopped putting myself down for that. So I hope you can love me for who I am."

Janny's lips quivered. She stood up and walked toward me. I came to meet her halfway around the dining table.

She put her arms around me. "Don't ever doubt that I love you," she whispered.

"Even if I'm a songwriter?"

"Even if you're a songwriter." She brushed a loose strand of hair out of my face, tucking it behind my ear. "I may not always understand you, I may not always know what to say to you or how to say it, but I always love you."

I sensed that Janny was a little embarrassed at what for her was an outpouring of emotion, so I gave her a peck on the cheek and let her return to her chair.

"I met Luke during the Bernie episode," she informed Jules. "He's the son of George Silver, Bernie's ex-partner."

"His mother was Dulcie Brown," I added. "He just found out about that recently."

There was a beat of silence.

"I can't wait to hear about that," Jeff proclaimed.

THAT SUMMER WOULD BRING violence in Mississippi, more sit-ins at lunch counters across the South, and on August twenty-eighth, the march on Washington. I didn't know it then, but Luke and I would be going together. We would listen to Dr. King's "I Have a Dream" speech, holding hands in the crowd on that hot and humid day in D.C. In a way, we felt we were already living the dream: a half-Negro boy and a white Jewish girl in love.

But we also knew that there were so many who weren't as lucky as we were.

Janny and Jules would worry about me taking that trip with Luke, as they'd worried about me when I'd first told them about my job in the Brill Building. But they knew they couldn't stop me from going, from doing what I believed in.

And it was then, on that day, we added another unbreakable rule to the Green family list.

4. Any rule can be broken if the reason is right. Sometimes there's no other choice.

aCKNOWLDGMeNTS

I aM eTerNaLLY GraTeFUL to my editor, Dan Ehrenhaft of Soho Teen, who read a manuscript of mine and liked it enough to think it would be a good idea for me to write a new mystery about the Brill Building. His patience, understanding, creative smarts, objectivity and general "good guyness" qualify him for publishing sainthood. "Saint Soho" does have a ring to it.

My deepest gratitude to my friend and legal advisor, Robin Sax, who always found the time to tell me the "emmes" (Yiddish word for "truth") of the law and to calm me down when it wasn't what I wanted to hear. Any legal mistakes in this book are mine, not hers.

Endless appreciation to my wonderful friend, amazing writer, and brilliant teacher, Julie Sayres, who is as generous with her ideas as she is with her loving heart.

Thanks for the memories to Brooks Arthur. Without his power of recall and open heart, this book could never have been written.

To my "computer guy" and friend, Gary Zembow, thanks for always being there day and night, to save the words.

I must acknowledge my dearest, darling husband, Barry Mann, who was no help whatsoever in writing this book, but who wrote incredible melodies for my words, and that's what made a few people interested in what this lyricist had to say when she turned to prose. He was and is still invaluable in other areas of my life that are very important. I thank him for being my guy and love him more every day.

Attention must be paid and thanks given to the late great Leopold Mann, the most beautiful German Shepherd in the world who spent his first six years tied to a dog house and his last two years being loved and loving us with his gigantic German Shepherd heart. He filled me with joy every moment that we shared. Leo watched this book being written and waited patiently each day for me to complete my work so we could go to the dog park. I will miss him forever.